The Gambler

FYODOR DOSTOYEVSKY

The Gambler

FYODOR DOSTOYEVSKY

FROM THE DIARY OF A YOUNG MAN

ARCTURUS

ARCTURUS

This edition published in 2013 by Arcturus Publishing Limited
26/27 Bickels Yard, 151–153 Bermondsey Street,
London SE1 3HA

Edited by George Davidson
Introduction by Charlotte Gerlings
Typesetting by Palimpsest Book Production Limited
Cover image: *La Salle du Jeu* (*The Games Room*), 1889, by Jean Beraud
(1849–1935). The Art Archive/Musée Carnavalet Paris/Gianni Dagli Orti.

ISBN: 978-1-84837-888-9
AD001860EN

Printed in the UK

Introduction

Fyodor Dostoyevsky was born in Moscow on 11 November 1821, the second of seven children. His father was an army surgeon and the family lived in an apartment at the Mariinsky Hospital for the Poor. As a child, Fyodor would sit beside the patients in the hospital gardens and listen to their stories, so that he grew up with strong empathy for the poor and oppressed.

At the Institute of Military Engineering in St Petersburg, he had the chance to study literature as well as science and mathematics. When he graduated in 1841, he immediately began writing and published his first novel, *Poor Folk* (1846), to critical acclaim.

In 1848, Dostoyevsky joined a literary and political group led by Mikhail Petrashevsky. Such groups were illegal in Tsarist Russia and in 1849 the Petrashevsky Circle – Dostoyevsky included – were accused of subversion and brought before a firing squad. At the very last minute they were *reprieved* and sentenced to hard labour in Siberia instead; it was a horrifying experience that haunted the author for ever.

After his release from prison camp, Dostoyevsky finally returned to St Petersburg in 1859 and to journalism and fiction; *The House of the Dead* appeared in 1862. But misfortune struck in 1864 with the deaths of both his wife and his brother, leaving Dostoyevsky with several dependent children – and huge gambling debts. The author's addiction inspired his novella *The Gambler* (1867), which was written in less than a month, in response to threats from his publisher to deprive him of his copyright.

Simultaneously, Dostoyevsky managed to produce one of his major masterpieces, *Crime and Punishment* (1867). There followed *The Idiot* (1869), *The Possessed* (1872) and his epic *The Brothers Karamazov* (1880).

Fyodor Dostoyevsky died on 9 February 1881 at his home in St Petersburg.

EDITOR'S PREFACE

The text that is published here is not a new translation of Dostoyevsky's novel *Игрок* ('Igrok', *The Gambler*), but a revision of the translation made by C. J. Hogarth, a translation which, whatever its merits in the past, had now, it was felt, become too dated in style and vocabulary to be able any longer to do justice to Dostoyevsky's work. The revision has, nonetheless, involved much more than a mere modernization of Hogarth's language. There has been constant recourse to the novel in its original Russian, and in many places where Hogarth's translation was judged not to reflect Dostoyevsky's words or meaning sufficiently closely, the text has been amended accordingly.

Since some of the characters in the novel are French, and others are Russians who (as was typical of the time) have a command of French, there are throughout the novel many short passages of comment or conversation in French or a mixture of French and Russian. There are also one or two very short passages in German. In Russian editions of the novel, these sections of French and German are found translated into Russian in footnotes; in this edition, they are translated into English in notes to be found at the end of the book. (In a few instances, where the context makes it absolutely clear what is meant, no translation has been given.) A few other notes have been provided to elucidate references to people, places or things the modern reader might not be familiar with.

Dostoyevsky's *The Gambler* was written and published in 1866. Dictated to a young stenographer Anna Gigorevna Snitkina (who soon after became Dostoyevsky's second wife), the book was written in twenty-six days during the month of October, in a desperate, but successful, attempt to meet a deadline of 1 November, failure to do which would have incurred severe financial penalties for the writer. While the novel is by no means autobiographical, certain aspects of it are closely related to Dostoyevsky's own life and experience. An addiction to gambling was, for example, something that Dostoyevsky knew well (he gambled for the first time in the German spa town of Wiesbaden in 1863, and continued to play throughout the 1860s, often losing heavily; he appears, however, to have lost his gambling mania in 1871), and the descriptions of the scenes in the roulette salons and of the players' and onlookers' behaviour and emotions must be based on first-hand knowledge.

Some of the characters of the novel, too, are surely not unrelated to those Dostoyevsky would have met in Wiesbaden, Homburg, Baden-Baden and elsewhere. One character, Polina Alexandrovna, is clearly based, both in name and behaviour, on Apollinaria (Polina) Suslova, a young woman with whom Dostoyevsky was for a time infatuated. And in Alexei Ivanovich, the eponymous gambler and narrator of the story, one must see reflections of Dostoyevsky the gambler and forlorn lover himself. For instance, Alexei's stated belief at the end of the book – 'All I need to do is play cautiously and patiently at first and the rest will follow. All I need to do is keep control of myself for one hour, and my destiny will be changed forever' – closely mirrors the recipe for success in gambling that Dostoyevsky proposed in a letter he wrote from Wiesbaden to a friend in 1863.

While perhaps less well known than other works by Dostoyevsky such as *Crime and Punishment*, *The Idiot* or *The Brothers Karamazov*, *The Gambler* is a masterpiece that is well worthy of inclusion among the classic works of world literature.

George Davidson

I

I have at last returned from my two weeks' leave of absence. My patron and his group arrived in Roulettenburg three days ago. The welcome I got from them was rather different to what I had expected. The General eyed me coldly, greeted me rather haughtily and then dismissed me to pay my respects to his sister. It was clear that they had acquired money from *somewhere*. I thought I could even detect a certain shame-facedness in the way the General looked at me. Maria Philippovna, too, seemed distracted, and hardly said a word to me. Nevertheless, she accepted the money I handed to her, counted it and listened to what I had to tell her. There were guests expected for dinner: Mezentsov, and the little Frenchman, and some Englishman or other; whenever there is money to hand, there's always a banquet, in the Muscovite style. Polina Alexandrovna, on seeing me, inquired why I had been away so long. Then, without waiting for an answer, she quite deliberately walked off. I clearly need to sort out what's going on. Something has developed.

I had been assigned a small room on the third floor of the hotel (for, as everyone here knows, I belong to the General's suite). It seems to me that the party has already gained some notoriety in the place, and the General is considered to be a Russian nobleman of great wealth. Even before dinner he asked me, among other things, to get two thousand-franc notes changed for him. This I did at the hotel desk, which will make people look on us as millionaires – for the next week anyway! Later, I was about to take Misha and Nadia for a walk when, as I was coming down the staircase, I was summoned to the General. He began by inquiring of me where I was going to take the children; and as he did so, I could see that he couldn't look me in the eye. He *wanted* to, but each time he was met with such a hard, disrespectful stare from me that he gave up in confusion. In pompous language, however, piling one sentence on to another and eventually losing the thread of what he was saying altogether, he gave me to understand that I was to take the children right away from the casino and out into the park. Finally, his temper exploded, and he added sharply: 'I suppose you might prefer to take them to the casino to play roulette? Pardon me for speaking so plainly, but I know how addicted you are to gambling. Although I'm not your mentor, nor have any wish to be, at least I have the right to demand that you do not actually compromise me.'

'I have no money for gambling,' I replied quietly. 'In order to lose money, you need to have some in the first place.'

'But you'll have some soon,' retorted the General, going a little red as he rummaged in his writing-desk and then consulted a memorandum book. Apparently he owed me a hundred and twenty roubles.

'Let's work this out,' he went on. 'We need to convert these roubles into thalers. Here, take a hundred thalers as a round sum. The rest will be safe with me.'

I took the money in silence.

'You mustn't be offended by what I say,' he continued. 'You're too touchy about these things. What I've said, I have said merely as a warning. To do so is no more than my right.'

When returning home with the children before dinner, I met a real cavalcade – our party were riding out to view some ruins. Two splendid carriages, drawn by magnificent horses, with Mademoiselle Blanche, Maria Philippovna and Polina Alexandrovna in one of them; the Frenchman, the Englishman and the General were accompanying them on horseback. The passers-by stopped to stare at them, for the effect was stunning – the General couldn't have done it better. I reckoned that, with the four thousand francs I had brought with me, added to what my patrons seemed already to have acquired, the party must have at least seven or eight thousand francs – though that would barely be enough for Mademoiselle Blanche, who, with her mother and the Frenchman, was also lodging in our hotel. The latter gentleman is called 'Monsieur le Comte' by the footmen, and Mademoiselle Blanche's mother is 'Madame la Comtesse'. Perhaps they really *are* a count and countess.

I knew that 'Monsieur le Comte' would take no notice of me when we met at dinner, and that the General would not dream of introducing us or of recommending me to him. But the Comte has lived a while in Russia, and knows that someone who is referred to as an 'uchitel'[1] is a pretty insignificant person. Of course, strictly speaking, he knows me perfectly well. I was an uninvited guest at the dinner – the General had forgotten to make the arrangements or else I would have been dispatched to dine at the *table d'hôte*[2]. When I turned up of my own accord, the General looked at me disapprovingly. Kind Maria Philippovna at once pointed to a place for me, but it was my having previously met the Englishman, Mr Astley, that saved the day, and from then on I counted as one of the company.

I had first met this strange Englishman in Prussia, where we had happened to be sitting facing one another on a train I was travelling in to catch up with our party; later, I had run across him in France, and again in Switzerland – twice in the space of two weeks! To think, therefore, that I should suddenly meet up with him again here in Roulettenburg! Never in my life had I known a shyer man; he was ridiculously shy, but he was well aware of that (he was no fool). At the same time, he was a gentle, amiable sort of a fellow, and even on our first encounter in Prussia I had managed to draw him out and he had told me that he had just been to the North Cape and was now anxious to visit the fair at Nizhny Novgorod. How he had come to make the General's acquaintance I don't know, but it seems to me he is absolutely smitten by Polina. Anyhow, he was delighted that I should sit next him at table, as he seems to look on me as his bosom friend.

During the meal the Frenchman put on airs; he was offhand and pompous to everyone. In Moscow too, I remember, he used to talk a lot of hot air. He droned on and on about finance and Russian politics, and though at times the General ventured to contradict him, he did so quietly so as not to totally lose his own dignity.

For myself, I was in an odd frame of mind. Even before the dinner was half over, I had asked myself the same old question: '*Why* do I continue to dance attendance on the General, instead of leaving him and his family long ago?' Every now and then I would glance at Polina Alexandrovna, but she paid no attention to me, until eventually I got so irritated that I decided to be a bit boorish.

First of all I suddenly, and for no reason whatever, loudly butted into the general conversation. More than anything, I wanted to pick a quarrel with the Frenchman; and with that end in view, I turned to the General and exclaimed in an overbearing sort of way – indeed, I think I actually interrupted him – that it had been almost impossible that summer for a Russian to dine anywhere at *tables d'hôte*. The General looked at me in astonishment.

'If you have any self-respect,' I went on, 'you risk abuse by doing so and are forced to put up with insults of every kind. Both at Paris and on the Rhine, and even in Switzerland, there are so many Poles, with their sympathisers, the French, at these *tables d'hôte* that you cannot get a word in edgeways if you happen to be merely a Russian.'

This I said in French. The General looked at me in confusion, not knowing whether to be angry or merely surprised that I should so far forget myself.

'Well, at least someone has taught you something somewhere,' said the Frenchman in a careless, contemptuous sort of tone.

'In Paris, too, I had an argument with a Pole,' I continued, 'and then with a French officer who supported him. But later some of the Frenchmen present took my side, as soon as I told them the story of how I once threatened to spit into a Monsignor's coffee.'

'To spit into it?' said the General in a tone of grave disapproval and with a look of astonishment, while the Frenchman looked at me in disbelief.

'Absolutely,' I replied. 'Once, when I had been feeling sure for two days that at any moment I might have to leave for Rome on business, I went round to the Embassy of the Holy See in Paris to have my passport visaed. There I encountered a sacristan of about fifty, a withered man with a frosty look. After listening politely but with no great enthusiasm to what I had to say, this sacristan asked me to wait a moment. I was in a hurry to leave, but of course I sat down, took out a copy of a French newspaper, the *Opinion Nationale*, and started reading an extraordinary piece of invective against Russia which happened to be in it. As I was occupying myself in this way, I heard someone enter an adjoining room and ask for Monsignor; after which I saw the sacristan make a low bow to the visitor, and then bow again as the visitor left. I ventured to remind the good man of my own business, whereupon, with an expression of, if anything, even greater chilliness, he again asked me to wait. Soon another visitor (some Austrian or other) arrived who, like myself, had come on business; and just as soon as he had stated his errand, he was taken upstairs! This made me very angry. I got up, went over to the sacristan and told him that, since Monsignor was receiving callers, he might just as well deal with my business too. At this, the sacristan shrank back in astonishment. It was simply beyond his understanding that any insignificant Russian should dare to compare himself with other visitors of Monsignor's! In a tone of the utmost effrontery, as though he were delighted to have the chance to insult me, he looked me up and down, and then shouted: "Do you suppose that Monsignor is going to put aside his coffee for *you*?" But I shouted even louder: "Let me tell you, I'm going to *spit* into that coffee! Yes, and if you don't get me my passport stamped with a visa this very minute, I'll take it to Monsignor myself."

"'What? While he's busy with the Cardinal?" screeched the sacristan, again recoiling in horror. Then, rushing to the door, he spread out his arms as though he would rather die than let me enter.

'At that point, I declared that I was a heretic and a barbarian. "Je suis hérétique et barbare," I said, and told him that archbishops and cardinals and monsignors, and all the rest of them, meant nothing to me. In a word, I showed him that I was not going to give way. He looked at me with an air of deep resentment. Then he snatched up my passport, and took it upstairs. A minute later, the passport had been stamped with the visa! Here it is now, if you care to see it,' I said, pulling out the document and showing them the visa for Rome.

'But . . .' the General began.

'What really saved you was the fact that you proclaimed yourself a heretic and a barbarian,' remarked the Frenchman with a smile. 'Cela n'était pas si bête.'[3]

'But is that how Russians ought to be treated? Why, when they come here, they don't dare say a word – they're even ready to deny that they're Russians at all! At all events, at my hotel in Paris I received far more attention from the other guests after I had told them about the set-to with the sacristan. The fat Polish nobleman who had been the most offensive of all those who were present at the *table d'hôte* faded into the background, while the Frenchmen were willing to put up with it when I told them that two years ago I had come across a man who, in 1812, a French soldier had shot at just because he wanted to fire his rifle at something. The man had been a boy of ten at the time, and his family had been unable to get out of Moscow.'

'Impossible!' spluttered the Frenchman. 'No French soldier would fire at a child!'

'Nevertheless, that's what happened,' I replied. 'It was a very respected retired captain who told me the story, and I myself could see the scar on his cheek.'

The Frenchman then began talking volubly. The General was going to support him, but I recommended that he read, for example, extracts from the *Memoirs* of General Perovsky[4], who, in 1812, had been a prisoner in the hands of the French. Finally Maria Philippovna said something to change the subject. The General was furious with me for having started the argument with the Frenchman. On the other hand, Mr Astley seemed to take great pleasure in my brush with Monsieur, and, rising from the table, suggested that we should have a drink together. The same evening, I managed to have a quarter of an hour's conversation with Polina Alexandrovna, and the talk soon extended to a stroll. We went into the park and walked towards the casino, and Polina sat down on a bench near the fountain and sent Nadia off to play with some other children. I told Misha to go and play by the fountain as well, and in this fashion we – that is to say, Polina and myself – contrived to find ourselves alone.

Of course, we began by talking about business matters. Polina was furious when I only handed her seven hundred gulden, because she had been expecting that, as the proceeds of pawning her diamonds, I would be bringing her at least two thousand gulden from Paris, or even more.

'Come what may, I *must* have money,' she said. 'And I'll get it somehow, otherwise I'll be ruined.'

I asked her what had happened during my absence.

'Nothing much, except two pieces of news that have reached us from St Petersburg. First of all, Grandmother is very ill and unlikely to last another couple of days. We had this news from Timofei Petrovich himself, and he's reliable. At any moment we're expecting to receive news of the end.'

'So you're all breathless with anticipation?' I asked.

'Of course, all of us, every minute of the day. We've been waiting for this for a year and a half now.'

'Waiting for it?'

'Yes, waiting for it. I'm not her blood relation, you know – I'm merely the General's step-daughter – but I'm sure the old lady has remembered me in her will.'

'Yes, I'm sure you'll come in for a good sum,' I said confidently.

'Yes, because she's fond of me. But how is it that *you* think so?'

I answered this question with another one. 'That Marquis of yours,' I said, 'is *he* familiar with your family secrets too?'

'Why are *you* so interested in all this?' she asked, looking at me coldly and severely.

'Never mind. If I'm not mistaken, the General has managed to borrow money from the Marquis.'

'Perhaps he has.'

'Is it likely that the Marquis would have lent him the money if he had not known something or other about Grandmother? And did you notice that three times during dinner, when talking about her, he called her "Dear Granny". What intimate, loving behaviour, to be sure!'

'Yes, that's true. Just as soon as he learns that I have inherited something from her, he will start to court me. Is that what you wanted to know?'

'Begin his courting? Why, I thought he'd been doing that for ages!'

'You *know* he hasn't,' retorted Polina angrily. Then, after a pause: 'But where on earth did you pick up this Englishman?'

'I knew you would ask about him.' So I told her of my previous encounters with Astley while I had been on my travels.

'He's very shy,' I said, 'and prone to falling in love. And he's in love with you already.'

'Yes, he is in love with me,' she replied.

'And he's ten times richer than the Frenchman. In fact, what *does* the Frenchman have? To me, it seems at least open to doubt that he has any possessions at all.'

'Oh, no, there's no reason to doubt it, he does have some chateau or other. Last night the General told me that for certain. *Now* are you satisfied?'

'Nevertheless, if I were you I would marry the Englishman.'

'Why?' asked Polina.

'Because, though the Frenchman is the handsomer of the two, he is also more disreputable, whereas the Englishman is not only a man of honour, but ten times the wealthier of the two.'

'Yes? But then the Frenchman is a marquis, and the cleverer of the two,' remarked Polina imperturbably.

'Is that so?' I said.

'Yes, absolutely.'

Polina was not at all pleased at my questioning. I could see she was doing her best to irritate me with the brusqueness of her answers, but I took no notice.

'It amuses me to see you getting angry,' she said. 'However, since I am allowing you to indulge in these questions and conjectures, you ought to pay me something for the privilege.'

'I consider I have a perfect right to put these questions to you,' I replied calmly, 'because I'm ready to pay for them, and also because I really don't care what becomes of me.'

Polina burst out laughing.

'The last time we were on the Schlangenberg, you told me that at one word from me you would be ready to throw yourself a thousand feet down the abyss. Some day I may remind you of what you said, just to see if you'll be as good as your word. Yes, you can be sure I shall do so. I hate you because I have allowed you to get away with so much, and I also hate you, and hate you all the more, because you are so necessary to me. For the time being I need you, so I have to spare you.'

Then she made as if to stand up. She had been sounding very angry. Indeed, of late her talks with me had invariably ended on a note of temper and malice. Yes, real malice.

'May I ask you who this Mademoiselle Blanche is?' I inquired (since I didn't want Polina to leave without an explanation).

'You *know* who she is – just Mademoiselle Blanche. Nothing more has happened lately. Probably she will soon be Madame General – that is to say, if the rumours that Grandmother is nearing her end should prove true. Mademoiselle Blanche, with her mother and her cousin, the Marquis, know very well that, as things stand at the moment, we're ruined.'

'And is the General in love at last?'

'That has nothing to do with it at the moment. Now, listen to me. Take these seven hundred florins[5], and go and play roulette with them. Win as much as you can for me, because I'm badly in need of money.'

So saying, she called Nadia to come and went back to the casino, where she joined the rest of our party. For myself, deep in thought and bewilderment, I took the first path to the left. It was as if something had struck me on the head when she told me to go and play roulette. Strangely enough, that something also seemed to make me hold back, and to set me to analysing my feelings with regard to her. In fact, during the two weeks of my absence I had felt far more at my ease than I did now on the day of my return, although while travelling I had moped around like an idiot or else rushed around feverishly, and had actually dreamt about her. Indeed, on one occasion (this happened in Switzerland, when I was asleep on the train) I had spoken aloud to her, which made all my fellow-travellers laugh. So once again I asked myself the question 'Do I or do I not love her?', and once again I couldn't answer my question or, rather, I told myself for the hundredth time that I loathed her. Yes, I loathed her; there were times (especially at the close of our chats together) when I would happily have given half my life to strangle her! I swear that if at such moments there had been a sharp knife within reach, I would have seized that knife with pleasure and plunged it into her breast. Yet I also swear that if, on the Schlangenberg, she really *had* said to me, 'Jump into that abyss,' I would have leapt into it with equal pleasure. Yes, that I knew perfectly well. One way or another, this business had to be settled soon. In some amazing way, she knew that too; the thought that I was fully conscious of her inaccessibility, and of the impossibility of my ever realising my dreams, afforded her, I am certain, the keenest possible pleasure. Otherwise, is it likely that she, cautious and clever woman that she was, would have indulged in this familiarity and openness with me? Up till that point, it seems to me, she had looked on me in the same way that that Empress in ancient times looked on her slave – the Empress who never bothered about undressing in front of a slave because she didn't think of a slave as a man. Yes, Polina must often have taken me for something less than a man!

Still, she had given me a job to do – to win what I could at roulette. Yet all the time I couldn't help wondering *why* it was so necessary for her to win something, and what new schemes could have been born in her ever-fertile brain. A host of new and unknown factors seemed to have arisen during the past two weeks, and it was up to me to discover them and investigate them, and to do so as soon as possible. But not now. What I had to do for the time being was head for the roulette table.

II

I admit I didn't like it. Although I had made up my mind to play, I felt averse to doing so on behalf of someone else. In fact, it rather upset my composure, and I entered the gaming-rooms feeling angry. At first glance, the whole scene irritated me. Never at any time have I been able to bear the servility which one meets in the world's press, but more especially in Russian newspapers, where, almost every spring, journalists write about two subjects in particular, namely the splendour and luxury of the casinos in the towns along the Rhine and the piles of gold that are to be seen lying on the gaming-tables. Those journalists aren't paid for doing this: they write this sort of stuff merely out of a spirit of disinterested obsequiousness. Because there's nothing splendid about the establishments at all, and not only are there no heaps of gold to be seen lying on their tables, there's very little money to be seen at all. Of course, during the season, some madman or another may make his appearance, generally an Englishman, or an Asiatic – a Turk, say – and (as happened during the summer of which I am writing) suddenly win or lose a great deal; but, as for the rest of the crowd, they only play for paltry sums, and there is seldom much money on the tables.

When, on the present occasion, I entered the gaming-rooms (for the first time in my life), it was some time before I could even make up my mind to play. For one thing, the crowd oppressed me. Had I been playing for myself, I think I would have left at once and never have embarked on gambling at all; my heart was thumping, and my mind was anything but composed. I knew, indeed had long ago made up my mind, that I would never leave Roulettenburg until some radical, some definitive, change had taken place in my fortunes. So it must be, and so it would be. No matter how ridiculous it may seem to you that I was expecting to win at roulette, I consider the generally accepted opinion that it is foolish and absurd to hope to win at gambling even more absurd. For why is gambling in any way worse than any other method of acquiring money? How, for instance, is it worse than trade? True, out of a hundred people only one can win, but what do I care about that?

At all events, I confined myself at first to simply looking on, and decided to attempt nothing serious. Indeed, I felt that if I began to do anything at all, I should do it in an absent-minded, haphazard sort of way – that's what I had in mind. What's more, I needed to learn the game itself, since, despite the thousand descriptions of roulette that I had read avidly, I knew nothing of its rules and had never even seen it played.

In the first place, everything about it seemed so sordid – morally nasty and dirty, that is. I'm not talking about the expectant, restless folk who, in their scores – even in their hundreds – could be seen crowded around the gaming-tables, because I can see nothing sordid in a desire to win quickly and win a lot. I have always applauded the opinion of a certain well-fed and well-off moralist who replied to someone's excuse that 'they only gambled for small stakes' by saying 'So much the worse, since that's just petty greed'.

Small-scale greed and massive greed amount to the same thing. It's all a matter of proportion. What might seem a small sum to a Rothschild might be a large sum to me. As for winnings, it's not just at roulette that people can be found depriving their fellow beings of something, it's everywhere. As to whether stakes and winnings are, in themselves, immoral is another question altogether, and I have no wish to express an opinion on that now. But the very fact that I had a strong desire to win made this gambling for gain, in spite of its attendant squalor, to have in my eyes – what should I say? – something intimate, something attractive about it: it's always pleasant to see people dispensing with ceremony and behaving openly and naturally with one another. Why deceive oneself? I could see that the whole thing was a futile and mindless pursuit. What, at first glance, seemed to me the ugliest feature about this mob of roulette players was the respect they showed for their occupation – the seriousness, and even the humility, with which they stood around the gaming-tables. Moreover, I had always drawn sharp distinctions between a game which is *de mauvais genre*[6] and a game which is permissible to a respectable person. In fact, there are two sorts of gambling – namely, the gambling of the gentleman and the gambling of the plebs, that is, gambling for gain, the gambling of the *hoi polloi*. Here, as I have said, I draw a clear distinction. Yet how essentially contemptible this distinction is! For instance, a gentleman may stake, say, five or ten *louis d'or*[7] – seldom more, unless he is a very rich man, when he may stake, say, a thousand francs – but he must do this simply for the love of the game itself, simply for sport, simply in order to observe the process of winning or losing, and, above all, as a man who remains quite uninterested in the possibility of coming out a winner. If he wins, he is at liberty, say, to laugh or pass a remark on the circumstance to a bystander, or place a stake again, or double his stake, but even this he must do solely out of curiosity and for the pleasure of watching the play of chances and calculations, and not from any vulgar desire to win. In a word, he must look on the gaming-table, on roulette or trente-et-quarante, as mere relaxations which have been arranged solely for his amusement. He must have no awareness of the greed and stratagems on which the bank is founded and maintained. Best of all, he ought to imagine his fellow-gamblers and the rest of the crowd who stand trembling over a coin to be as rich and gentlemanly as himself and playing solely for recreation and pleasure. This complete ignorance of the realities, this innocent view of mankind, is what, in my opinion, constitutes the true aristocrat. For instance, I have even seen doting mothers so far indulge their innocent, elegant daughters – young ladies of fifteen or sixteen – as to give them a few gold coins and teach them how to play; and whether the young ladies have won or lost, they have invariably laughed and walked away as though they were well pleased.

In the same way, I once saw our General approach the table in a solid, dignified manner. A flunkey dashed to offer him a chair, but the General didn't even notice him. Slowly he took out his money bags, and equally slowly took out three hundred francs in gold, which he staked on the black, and won. But he didn't lift his winnings – he left them there on the table. Again the ball landed on black, and again he didn't pick up what he had won; and when, the third time, the ball landed on *red* he lost, at a stroke, twelve hundred francs. Yet even then he stood up with a smile, and so preserved his reputation. But I know he was raging inwardly and had the stake been two or three times as much as it was, he would not have been able to stop himself giving vent to his disappointment. On the other hand, I saw a Frenchman first win, and then lose, thirty thousand francs, cheerfully and without a murmur. Yes, even if a gentleman should lose his whole fortune, he must never give way to anger. Money must be so far beneath a gentlemen as never to be worth a thought. Of course, the *supremely* aristocratic thing is to be entirely oblivious of the rabble and all one's surroundings, but sometimes it may be just as aristocratic to adopt the opposite course and to notice, and even gaze at, the mob (preferably through a lorgnette), as though one were taking the crowd and its squalor for some sort of spectacle that has been organised specially for a gentleman's diversion. Though you may be jostled by the crowd, you must look as though you are quite sure you are just an observer, having nothing to do with those you are observing. At the same time, to look too attentively is also unbecoming to a gentleman, seeing that no spectacle is worth a long look – there are no spectacles in the world which merit too close an inspection from a gentleman.

However, to me personally the scene *did* seem to be worth undisguised attention, more especially in view of the fact that I had come there not only to look at the crowd, but also sincerely and wholeheartedly to become part of it. As for my private moral views, there was no room for them amongst my actual practical viewpoint. Let's leave it at that for the time being: I'm only writing this to relieve my conscience. But let me also say this: that I have recently had an intense aversion to any testing of my actions and thoughts by any moral standard. There is another standard altogether that has been directing my life . . .

As a matter of fact, the crowd does play quite dishonestly. Indeed, I would even go so far as to say that there is a good deal of sheer robbery going on around a gaming-table. The croupiers who sit at the two ends of it have not only to watch the stakes but also to calculate the winnings – a huge amount of work for two men. As for the crowd itself, well, it consists mostly of Frenchmen. But I wasn't taking notes merely in order to be able to give you a description of roulette, but so as to get my bearings with regard to my behaviour when I myself would begin to play. For example, I noticed that very frequently someone would reach out and grab someone else's winnings when they had won. Then an argument would start, and frequently an uproar; and it would be a case of 'I beg you to prove, and to produce witnesses to the fact, that the stake was yours'.

At first the proceedings were all Greek to me. All I could guess or work out was that stakes were hazarded on numbers, on 'odd' or 'even', and on colours. Of Polina's money I decided to risk, that evening, only a hundred gulden. The thought that I was not going to be playing for myself quite unnerved me. It was an unpleasant feeling, and I tried hard to banish it. I had the notion that, once I began to play for Polina, I would ruin my own luck. I wonder if anyone has *ever* approached a gaming-table without falling an immediate prey to superstition? I began by pulling out fifty gulden, and staking them on 'even'. The wheel spun and stopped on 13. I'd lost! With a sick feeling in my stomach, just so that I could get out of the crowd and go home, I staked another fifty gulden, this time on the red. The ball landed on red. I next staked the hundred gulden just where they were lying, and again red won. Yet again I staked the whole sum, and again the red turned up. Clutching my four hundred gulden, I placed two hundred of them on the twelve middle numbers, to see what would come of it. The result was that the croupier paid me three times my total stake! Thus from one hundred gulden my stock had grown to eight hundred! At that point, such a strange, inexplicable, unusual feeling came over me that I decided to leave. The thought kept coming into my mind to me that if I had been playing for myself alone I would never have had luck like this. I staked the whole eight hundred gulden on 'even'. The wheel stopped at 4. I was paid out another eight hundred gulden, and, snatching up my pile of sixteen hundred gulden, I left in search of Polina Alexandrovna.

I found the whole party walking in the park, and I wasn't able to speak to her till after supper. This time the Frenchman was absent from the meal, and the General seemed to be in a more expansive vein. Among other things, he thought it necessary to remind me that he would be sorry to see me playing at the gaming-tables. In his opinion, such conduct would greatly compromise him, especially if I were to lose large sums. 'And even if you were to *win* a lot, I would still be compromised,' he added with a meaningful look. 'Of course I have no *right* to tell you what to do or not do, but you yourself will agree that . . .' As usual, he didn't finish his sentence. I answered drily that I had very little money, and that, consequently, even if I did gamble, I was hardly in a position to indulge in any conspicuous play. At last, when going up to my room, I managed to hand Polina her winnings, and told her that, next time, I wouldn't play for her.

'Why not?' she asked anxiously.

'Because I want to play *for myself*,' I replied, looking at her in surprise, 'and playing for you prevents me.'

'Are you so sure your roulette-playing will get you out of your difficulties?' she inquired with a quizzical smile.

I replied 'Yes' very seriously, and then added: 'My certainty about winning may perhaps seem ridiculous to you, but just let me do things my own way.'

Nonetheless she insisted that I share the day's winnings with her fifty-fifty, and offered me 800 gulden on condition that from then on I gambled only on those terms; but I refused once and for all, stating, as my reason, that I was quite unable to play on behalf of anyone else. 'I'm not unwilling to do so,' I said, 'but I would probably lose.'

'Well, absurd though it may be, I place great hopes on roulette,' she said ponderingly, 'so you *must* keep playing as my partner and on equal shares – and you will.'

Then she left me, not listening to any further objections from me.

III

The next day she didn't say a word to me about gambling. In fact, she deliberately avoided talking to me, although her manner towards me had not changed: she had the same calm coolness when she met me, a coolness mingled even with a hint of contempt and dislike. She is, quite simply, making no effort to conceal her dislike of me. That I can see plainly. At the same time, she doesn't trouble to conceal from me the fact that I am necessary to her, and that she is keeping me for some purpose she has in mind. Consequently, there has become established between us a relationship which to a large extent is quite incomprehensible to me, considering her general pride and aloofness towards everyone else. For example, she knows that I'm madly in love with her and allows me to speak to her of my passion (although she could not well show her contempt for me more than by permitting me, unhindered and unrebuked, to speak to her of my love). It is as if to say: 'You see how little regard I have for your feelings, as well as how little I care about what you say to me or your feelings for me.' Likewise, though she talks to me as before about her own affairs, it is never with complete frankness. In her contempt for me there are refinements. Although she knows perfectly well that I'm aware of certain circumstances in her life, of something which might one day cause her trouble, she talks to me about her affairs (whenever she has need of me for some purpose) as though I were a slave or a passing acquaintance – yet tells me only as much as one would need to know if one were going to be sent on an errand. Although I don't know the whole story and although she can see how much I am hurt and worried by her anxieties, she never thinks it worthwhile to reassure me with friendship and frankness – even though, since she not infrequently uses me to carry out errands for her that are not only troublesome but risky, she should, in my opinion, be completely frank with me. But she never seems to think it worth her while to trouble herself about *my* feelings, about the fact that I am anxious about her troubles and misfortunes, perhaps three times as much as she is herself.

For three weeks I had known of her intention to play roulette. She had even warned me that she would like me to play on her behalf, since it was unbecoming for her to play in person, and, from her tone I had gathered that there was something on her mind besides a mere desire to win money. As if money could matter to *her*! No, she had some end in view, and there were circumstances at which I could only guess but not know for certain. Of course, the state of slavery and humiliation in which she kept me might have afforded me, as such things often do, the possibility of questioning her freely (seeing that, inasmuch as I figured in her eyes as a mere slave and nonentity, she could not very well have taken offence at any brash curiosity on my part); but the fact was that, though she let me question her, she never gave me a single answer. Sometimes she didn't even notice the questions. That is how things stood between us.

The next day there was a lot of talk about a telegram which had been sent to St Petersburg four days earlier, but to which there had been no reply. The General was visibly disturbed and moody, because it had something to do with Grandmother. The Frenchman, too, was upset, and after dinner the whole party talked long and seriously together – the Frenchman's tone being extraordinarily haughty and offhand to everybody. It reminded me of the proverb, 'Invite a man to your table, and he'll soon put his feet on it.' Even to Polina he was brusque almost to the point of rudeness. Yet he still seemed glad to join us in our walks in the casino gardens or in our rides and drives about town. I had long been aware of certain circumstances which bound the General to him; I had long been aware that in Russia they had hatched some scheme together, although I didn't know whether the plot had come to anything or whether it was still only at the stage of being talked about. Likewise I was aware, in part, of a family secret – namely, that last year, the Frenchman had bailed the General out of debt and had given him 30,000 roubles to pay his Treasury dues on retiring from the service. And now, of course, the General is in his clutches. But the main part in the affair is being played by Mademoiselle Blanche. Of that I have no doubt.

But who *is* this Mademoiselle Blanche? They say she's a Frenchwoman of good birth who has both her mother and a colossal fortune here with her. It's also known that she is related in some way to the Marquis, but only distantly – a cousin or second cousin or something like that. Likewise I know that, before my journey to Paris, she and the Frenchman had behaved more formally and delicately towards the rest of our party, but that now their acquaintanceship has taken on a much more coarse and intimate character. Perhaps they think that our means are too modest for them, and, therefore, that we are unworthy of politeness or discretion. What's more, for the last three days I have noticed certain looks that Astley has been casting towards Mademoiselle Blanche and her mother, and it has occurred to me that he must have had some previous acquaintance with the two of them. I have even surmised that the Frenchman, too, must have met Mr Astley before. Astley is a man so shy, reserved and silent in his manner that one can be sure he'll be discreet. At all events the Frenchman accords him only the slightest of greetings, and scarcely even looks at him. Certainly he doesn't seem to be afraid of him, which is understandable enough. But why does Mademoiselle Blanche never look at the Englishman either? Particularly since, *a propos* of something or another, the Marquis remarked yesterday that the Englishman is without doubt immensely rich. Is that not a sufficient reason to make Mademoiselle Blanche look at him? Anyway, the General seems extremely uneasy and one can well understand what a telegram announcing his aunt's death would mean for him.

Although I thought it probable that Polina was avoiding conversation with me for a definite reason, I too adopted a cold and indifferent air, for I felt pretty certain that it would not be long before she approached me. For two days, therefore, I devoted my attention to Mademoiselle Blanche. The poor General was in despair! To fall in love at fifty-five, and with such ardour, is indeed a misfortune! And add to that the state of being a widower, his children, his ruined property, his debts, and the woman he had fallen in love with. Because, although Mademoiselle Blanche is extremely good-looking, she has one of those faces one is afraid of. At any rate, I myself have always been afraid of such women. Apparently about twenty-five years old, she is tall with broad, sloping shoulders; her neck and bosom are ample in their proportions; her skin is dull yellow in colour, while her hair (which is extremely abundant, enough to make two normal coiffures) is as black as Indian ink. Add to that a pair of black eyes with yellowish whites, an impudent look, gleaming teeth, lips which are always painted, and she smells of musk. As for her clothing, it is invariably rich, striking and chic, but in good taste. Lastly, her feet and hands are exquisite, and her voice is a deep contralto. Sometimes she laughs and shows her teeth, but generally she's taciturn and haughty – especially in the presence of Polina and Maria Philippovna. (There is a strange rumour going round that Maria Philippovna is leaving for Russia.) She seems to me almost totally lacking in education, and even intelligence, but she's cunning and suspicious. It seems to me, though, that her life has not been lacking in incident. Perhaps, if the truth were known, the Marquis is not her kinsman at all, and equally her mother not her mother, but there is evidence that, in Berlin, where we had first come across the two of them, they had acquaintances of good standing. As for the Marquis himself, I doubt to this day whether he is a Marquis – although there can be no doubt whatsoever that he has formerly belonged to high society (for instance, in Moscow and Germany). What he was in France, I have no idea. All I know is that he is said to own a chateau.

I've been expecting a lot to happen during the last two weeks, but I still don't know whether anything decisive has yet been agreed between Mademoiselle and the General. Everything seems to depend on our finances, on whether the General will be able to flourish sufficient money in her face. If ever the news should arrive that Grandmother is not dead, Mademoiselle Blanche will, I feel sure, disappear in a twinkling. It surprises and amuses me to observe what a passion for intrigue I'm developing. But how I loathe it all! I would happily abandon everybody and everything! But could I really leave Polina, could I really stop spying on those around her? Espionage is a contemptible thing, but what is that to me?

Mr Astley, too, I have found a curious person. I am quite sure he has fallen in love with Polina. It is remarkable and amusing to see how much can be read from the face of a shy and painfully humble man who has been touched with the divine passion, especially when he would rather sink into the earth than betray himself by a single word or look. Though Mr Astley frequently meets us when we are out walking, he merely takes off his hat and passes us by, though I know he is dying to join us. Even if invited to do so, he would refuse. Again, in places of amusement – in the casino, at concerts, or near the fountain – he's never far from the spot where we're sitting. In fact, *wherever* we are – in the park, in the forest or on the Schlangenberg – one need only look up and glance around to catch sight of at least *some* part of Mr Astley's body sticking out, whether on an adjacent path or behind a bush. Yet he never misses any opportunity to speak to me, and, one morning when we had met and exchanged a couple of words, he burst out in his usual abrupt way, without even saying good morning: 'That Mademoiselle Blanche. You know, I've seen a good many women like her.'

After that he was silent and looked me meaningfully. What he meant I don't know, but to my look of inquiry, he returned only a nod, and said 'It's true, you know.'

Presently, however, he resumed:

'Does Mademoiselle Polina like flowers?'

' I really cannot say,' was my reply.

'What? You cannot say?' he cried in great astonishment.

'No. I've never noticed whether she does or not,' I repeated with a smile.

'Hm! Then I've an idea in my mind,' he said. Then with a nod, he walked off, looking pleased.

Our conversations are always in abominable French.

IV

Today has been a day of folly, stupidity, absurdity! It's now eleven o'clock in the evening, and I'm sitting in my room, thinking. It all began this morning with my being forced to go and play roulette for Polina Alexandrovna. When she handed me her six hundred gulden, I insisted on two conditions – namely, that I would not go halves with her in her winnings, if any (that is to say, I wouldn't take anything for myself), and that she should explain to me, this very evening, why it was so necessary for her to win and how much she needed. Because I couldn't believe she was doing all this merely for the sake of money. Clearly she did need some money, and as soon as possible, and for a special purpose. Well, she promised to explain matters to me, and off I went. There was a tremendous crowd in the gaming-rooms. And what an arrogant, greedy crowd it was! I pushed forward towards the middle of the room until I had secured a seat at a croupier's elbow. Then I began to play rather timidly, venturing only twenty or thirty gulden at a time. Meanwhile, I watched and took notes. It seemed to me that calculation was superfluous and by no means had the importance that certain other players attached to it, sitting with sheets of paper in their hands on which they wrote down the wins and calculated the odds, finally placing bets – and losing in exactly the same way as we simpler mortals who played without any calculating at all.

However, I deduced from the scene one conclusion which seemed to me reliable – namely, that in the flow of fortuitous chances there is, if not a system, at all events a sort of order. This, of course, is very strange. For instance, a dozen middle numbers will always be followed by a dozen or so later ones. If the ball stops twice in the last dozen numbers, it will then move on to the first dozen, and then, again, to a dozen of the middle numbers, and drop into them three or four times, and then revert to the last dozen again; then, after another couple of rounds, the ball will again pass to the first numbers, land on them once, and then go back three times to the middle series, continuing like this for an hour and a half or two hours. One, three, two; one, three, two. It's all very strange. Again, for a whole day or a whole morning, the red will alternate with the black, but changing from one moment to the next almost without any order so that scarcely two consecutive turns end on the one colour or the other. Yet, the next day, or perhaps the next evening, the red alone will keep turning up in a run of over two score, and continue like that for quite a length of time – say, for a whole day. Most of these circumstances were pointed out to me by Mr Astley, who stood at the gaming-table the whole morning but never once placed a bet himself.

For myself, I lost all that I had on me, and very quickly. To begin with, I staked two hundred gulden on 'even', and won. Then I bet the same amount again, and won; and so on some two or three times. At one point I must have had in my hands – gathered within a space of five minutes – about four thousand gulden. That, of course, would have been the right time for me to have walked away, but there arose in me a strange feeling, as if I wanted to challenge Lady Luck, to slap her cheek and stick my tongue out at her. Accordingly I set down the largest stake allowed by the rules – four thousand gulden – and lost. Fired up by this mishap, I pulled out all the money I had left, staked it all on the same number as before and – lost again! Then I got up from the table, feeling stunned. What had happened to me I could barely comprehend, and only told Polina of my losses just before dinner. Before that, I just wandered about in the park.

At dinner I was as excited as I had been at the meal three days ago. Mademoiselle Blanche and the Frenchman were dining with us, and it appeared that the former had been to the casino that morning and had seen my exploits there. So now she showed me more attention when talking to me, while, for his part, the Frenchman approached me and asked outright if it had been my own money that I had lost. He appeared to be suspicious that there was something going on between Polina and myself. I lied, telling him that the money had been all my own.

At this the General seemed extremely surprised, and asked me where

I had got the money from, to which I replied that, although I had begun with only 100 gulden, six or seven rounds had increased my money to five or six thousand gulden, and that I had subsequently lost the whole lot in two more rounds.

All this, of course, was plausible enough. During my recital I glanced at Polina, but her face was blank. However, she had allowed me to lie without correcting me, and from that I concluded that she wanted me to lie and to hide the fact that I had been playing on her behalf. 'At all events,' I thought to myself, 'she, in her turn, has promised to give me an explanation tonight, and to reveal something or other to me.'

Although the General appeared to be taking stock of me, he said nothing. Yet I could see uneasiness and annoyance in his face. Perhaps his straitened circumstances made it hard for him to hear of piles of gold passing through the hands of an irresponsible fool like me in the space of quarter of an hour. Now, I have an idea that last night he and the Frenchman had a bit of a set-to. At all events they closeted themselves together, and then had a long and heated discussion, after which the Frenchman appeared to leave in a temper, to return early this morning to renew the argument. On hearing of my losses, however, he only remarked sharply, even spitefully, that 'a man ought to be more careful'. Then, for some reason or another, he added that, 'though a great many Russians go in for gambling, they're no good at it'.

'I think roulette was devised specially for Russians,' I retorted, and when the Frenchman smiled contemptuously at my reply, I remarked further that I was sure I was right, and more than that, that in talking about Russians as gamblers, I was criticising them more than praising them, so he could believe what I was saying.

'On what do you base your opinion?' he inquired.

'On the fact that to the virtues and merits of the civilised Westerner, there has, historically, been added – almost as his main virtue – a capacity for acquiring capital, whereas, not only is the Russian incapable of acquiring capital, but he also loses what he has wantonly and by sheer folly. Nonetheless, we Russians often need money, so we are glad of, and greatly devoted to, a method of acquiring it such as roulette, whereby one may grow rich in a couple of hours without doing any work. This method, I repeat, has a great attraction for us, but since we play recklessly, and without taking any trouble, we almost invariably lose.'

'To a certain extent that is true,' assented the Frenchman smugly.

'Oh no, it's not true at all,' interrupted the General sternly. 'And you,' he added, to me, 'you ought to be ashamed of yourself for belittling your own country!'

'I apologise,' I said. 'But it would be difficult to say which is the worse of the two – Russian ineptitude or the German method of growing rich through honest toil.'

'What an extraordinary idea,' exclaimed the General.

'And what a *Russian* idea!' added the Frenchman.

I smiled, because I was rather glad to be quarrelling with them.

'I would rather live a wandering life in a Kirghiz tent,' I cried, 'than bow the knee to the German idol!'

'*What* idol?' exclaimed the General, now seriously angry.

'The German method of amassing riches. I've not been here very long, but I can tell you that what I have seen and verified makes my Tatar blood boil. Good Lord! I have no wish for virtues of that sort. Yesterday I went for a walk, about six or seven miles, and everywhere I went I found that things are exactly as we read about them in edifying German picture-books – every house has its "Vater"[8], who is horribly virtuous and extraordinarily honest. So honest is he that it's terrifying to have anything to do with him. I can't bear people of that sort. Every such "Vater" has his family, and in the evenings they read improving books aloud. Over their roofs rustle elm-trees and chestnuts. The sun has sunk to its rest; a stork is roosting on the gable; and all is beautifully poetic and touching. Don't be angry, General. Let me tell you something that is even more touching than that. I can remember how, of an evening, my own father, now dead, used to sit under the lime-trees in his little garden and read books aloud to my mother and me. So I am in a position to comment on this sort of thing. But here every family is tied in slavery and submission to its "Vater". They work like oxen, and amass wealth like Jews. Suppose the "Vater" has put by a certain number of gulden which he hands over to his eldest son, in order that said son may acquire a trade or a small plot of land. Well, one result of that is to deprive the daughter of a dowry, and so leave her a spinster. For the same reason, the parents will have to sell the younger son into bondage or the army, in order that he may earn more towards the family capital. Yes, such things *are* done, I've been making inquiries on the subject. It's all done out of sheer rectitude – out of a rectitude that is exaggerated to the point of the younger son believing that it was *right* that he was sold (isn't it simply idyllic when the victim rejoices that he has been sacrificed?). What more do I want to say? Well, this: that these matters oppress the eldest son just as much. Perhaps he has his Gretchen, to whom his heart is bound; he can't marry her because he hasn't yet amassed sufficient gulden. So the pair wait on in a mood of sincere and virtuous expectation, and smilingly sacrifice themselves. Gretchen's cheeks grow sunken, and she begins to wither; until at last, after some twenty years, their wealth has increased, and sufficient gulden have been honourably and virtuously accumulated. Then the "Vater" blesses his forty-year-old heir and the thirty-five-year-old Gretchen with the sunken bosom and the scarlet nose, after which he bursts into tears, reads the pair a lesson on morality, and dies. In turn, the eldest son now becomes a virtuous "Vater", and the story begins all over again. In fifty, sixty or seventy years' time the grandson of the original "Vater" will have amassed a considerable sum; and that sum he will hand over to his son, and the latter to *his* son, and so on for generations, until at length a Baron Rothschild will arise, or a "Hoppe and Company"[9], or the devil knows what! Is it not a beautiful sight – the spectacle of a century or two of labour, patience, intellect, rectitude, character, perseverance and calculation, with a stork sitting on the roof above it all? What's more, they think there could never be anything better than this, and from that point of view they begin to judge the rest of the world and to censure all who are at fault – that is to say, who are not exactly like themselves. Yes, there you have it in a nutshell. For my own part, I would rather grow fat in the

Russian style or squander all I have at roulette. I have no wish to produce a "Hoppe and Company" five generations down the line. I want the money for *myself*, and I don't consider myself as inferior to, or in some way necessary for, making money. I may be wrong, but there you have it. That's what *I* think.'

'How far you're right in what you have said, I don't know,' remarked the General moodily, 'but I *do* know that you're becoming an insufferable drama-queen whenever you get the slightest chance to . . .'

As usual, he left his sentence unfinished. Indeed, whenever he embarked on anything that went anywhere beyond the limits of daily small-talk, he left what he was saying unfinished. The Frenchman had listened to me contemptuously, with a slight protruding of his eyes; but he couldn't have understood very much of my harangue. As for Polina, she had looked on with serene indifference. She seemed to have heard neither my voice nor any other during the meal.

V

Yes, she had been extraordinarily deep in her own thoughts. Yet, on leaving the table, she immediately ordered me to accompany her for a walk. We took the children with us, and set out for the fountain in the park.

I was in such an irritated frame of mind that I rudely and abruptly blurted out a question as to 'why our Marquis de Griers, our Frenchman, no longer accompanied her on her walks and didn't speak to her for days on end'.

'Because he's a brute,' she replied rather oddly. It was the first time I had heard her speak like that about De Griers, so I was momentarily awed into silence by this expression of resentment.

'Have you noticed, too, that today he is by no means on good terms with the General?' I went on.

'Yes, and I suppose you want to know why,' she replied irritably. 'You are aware, are you not, that the General is mortgaged to the Marquis, for all his property? Consequently, if the General's aunt doesn't die, the Frenchman will become the absolute owner of everything he now holds only in pledge.'

'Then it really is the case that everything is mortgaged? I've heard rumours to that effect, but was unaware to what extent they might be true.'

'Yes, they *are* true. So what?'

'Why, then it'll be a case of "Goodbye, Mademoiselle Blanche",' I remarked, 'because in such circumstances she would never become Madame General. Do you know, I believe the old man is so much in love with her that he might shoot himself if she dropped him. At his age it's a dangerous thing to fall in love.'

'Yes, something, I believe, *will* happen to him,' Polina agreed thoughtfully.

'And what a splendid thing this all is!' I continued. 'Could anything be more calculated to show that she has only agreed to marry for money? Not one of the decencies has been observed; the whole affair has taken place without the least ceremony. And as for Grandmother, what could be more comical, yet more sordid, than sending off telegram after telegram to find out if she's dead? What do you think, Polina Alexandrovna?'

'It's all nonsense,' she said with a shudder. 'So I'm all the more surprised that *you* should be so cheerful. What are *you* so pleased about? Is it because you've gone and lost my money?'

'What? The money you gave me to lose? I told you I would never manage to win for other people, least of all for you. I did as you asked simply because you ordered me to, but you mustn't blame me for the result. I warned you no good would come of it. Are you depressed at having lost your money? Why do you need so much?'

'Why are you asking me all these questions?'

'Because you promised to explain everything to me. Listen. I'm certain that, as soon as I begin to play for myself (and I still have a hundred and twenty gulden left), I'll start winning. You can then take what you need from me.'

She made a scornful grimace.

'You mustn't be angry with me for making such a proposal,' I continued. 'I'm so conscious of being only a nonentity in your eyes that you needn't mind accepting money from me. A gift from me couldn't possibly offend you. Moreover, it was me who lost your gulden.'

She glanced at me but, seeing that I was angry and being sarcastic, changed the subject.

'My affairs cannot possibly interest you,' she said. 'Still, if you *do* wish to know, I'm in debt. I borrowed some money and I must pay it back again. I have a strange, stupid idea that I am bound to win at the gaming-tables. Why I think so I cannot say, but I do think so, and with some assurance. Perhaps it's because of that assurance that I now find myself without any other resource.'

'Or perhaps it is because it is so *necessary* for you to win. It is like a drowning man clutching at a straw. You yourself will agree that, unless he was drowning, he wouldn't mistake a straw for the trunk of a tree.'

Polina looked surprised. 'What?' she said. 'Is it not the case that you too are hoping to gain something from gambling? Did you not tell me again and again, two weeks ago, that you were certain of winning at roulette if you played here? And did you not ask me not to consider you a fool for doing so? Were you joking? You can't have been, for I remember that you spoke with such seriousness that you obviously weren't joking.'

'True,' I replied gloomily. 'I always felt certain that I would win here. Indeed, what you say makes me ask myself: 'Why have my absurd, senseless losses today not raised a doubt in my mind?' Because I'm still positive that, just as soon as I begin to play for myself, I'll definitely win.'

'And why are you so certain?'

'To tell you the truth, I don't know. I only know that I must win, that it's the one resource I have left. Yes, why *do* I feel so sure about that?'

'Perhaps because one cannot help winning if one is fanatically certain of doing so.'

'Yet I bet you don't think me capable of serious feeling in the matter.'

'I don't care whether you are or not,' answered Polina with calm indifference. 'Well, since you ask me, I *do* doubt your ability to take anything seriously. You are capable of worrying, but not seriously. You are too flighty and unsettled a person for that. But why do you want money? Not a single one of the reasons you gave me then can be considered serious.'

'By the way,' I interrupted, 'you say you want to pay off a debt. It must be a large one. Is it to the Frenchman?'

'What do you mean by asking all these questions? You're being very clever today. You're not drunk, are you?'

'You know that you and I don't stand on ceremony, and that some-times I ask you very direct questions. I tell you again that I'm your slave, and slaves cannot cause shame or offence.'

'That's all nonsense! And I can't stand this "slave" theory of yours.'

'Be good enough to note that I am not speaking of this slavery of mine from any desire I have to be your slave. I speak of it as a fact, something that doesn't depend on me at all.'

'Tell me straight, why do you need money?'

'And you tell me why you need to know.'

'Oh well, as you please,' she said, tossing her head haughtily.

'You can't stand this "slave" theory of mine, but you still demand slavishness. "Answer me and don't argue", you say. Fine, so be it. What do I need money for, you ask? Why ask? Money is everything!'

'I understand that, but not someone getting into such a state of madness from wanting it. After all, you too are getting into a state of frenzy, or fatalism. There's something going on here, some special purpose. Tell me straight, without prevarication. That's what I want from you.'

She seemed to be getting angry, and I was really pleased to see her questioning me so heatedly.

'Of course there's a purpose, ' I said, 'but I don't know how to explain what it is. It's no more than that with money I would be a different man, even to you, and not a slave.'

How? How will you manage that?'

'You ask me how I will manage that? How is it that you can't even understand how I could make you look at me as something other than a slave? But that's something I don't want, this surprise and bewilderment.'

'You've been saying that you found this slavery a pleasure. And I thought so too.'

'You thought so too!' I exclaimed with a strange feeling of enjoyment. 'Oh, how delightful such naivety is coming from you! Well, yes, all right then, being your slave *is* a pleasure to me. There is, there is pleasure to be found in the highest degree of servility and humiliation!' I rambled on. 'The Devil only knows, there may also be in being knouted[10], when the knout lands on one's back and tears the flesh . . .

But perhaps I want to try other pleasures. It's not that long ago that the General, in your presence, lectured me about the seven hundred roubles a year which, it seems, I may still not get from him. And the Marquis de Griers, with raised eyebrows, stares at me and at the same time really doesn't take any notice of me at all. While perhaps I have a strong desire to pull the Marquis de Griers' nose in front of you.'

'That's just childish talk. It's always possible to behave with dignity. If you have a quarrel with someone, that should raise your standards, not lower them.'

'A maxim straight from the textbooks! Suppose I *cannot* behave with dignity? By that I mean that, although I do have self-respect, I don't know how to behave properly. Do you know why? It is because we Russians are too richly and variously gifted to be able to immediately find the proper mode of expression. It is all a question of form. Most of us are bountifully endowed with intellect but it also requires a touch of genius to choose the right form of behaviour. And we lack genius for the simple reason that so little genius exists at all. Only the French – well, perhaps a few other Europeans as well – have elaborated their formalities so well as to be able to seem to behave with great dignity and yet be completely undignified persons. That is why, with us, form is so all-important. The Frenchman may receive an insult – a real, venomous insult – but he will not so much as frown. But a tweaking of the nose he cannot bear, because such an act is an infringement of the accepted, of the time-honoured order of decorum. That is why our good ladies are so fond of Frenchmen – the Frenchman's manners, they say, are perfect! But in my opinion there is no such thing as a Frenchman's manners. All they have in them is the *coq gaulois* – the "French cockerel". However, as I'm not a woman, I don't properly understand this matter. Cocks may be excellent birds. But there I am, talking nonsense, and you're just letting me. You ought to stop and correct me more often when I'm speaking to you, for I am too apt to say anything and everything that's in my head. You see, I've lost my manners. I agree that I have none, nor any dignity either. I'll tell you why. I set no store on such things. Everything in me has been brought to a halt. You know the reason. I haven't a single human thought in my head. For a long while now I have been ignorant of what is going on in the world – here or in Russia. I've been to Dresden, yet have no idea what Dresden is like. You know the cause of my obsession. Since I have no hope now, and am a mere cipher in your eyes, I will tell you outright that wherever I go I see only you – all the rest is a matter of indifference. Why or how I have come to love you, I do not know. Maybe you are not particularly attractive to look at. Do you know, I am quite ignorant even as to what your face is like. In all probability, too, your heart is not very attractive, and it's possible that your mind is wholly ignoble.'

'And because you do not believe in my nobility of mind, you think to purchase me with money?' she said.

'*When* have I thought to do so?' was my reply.

'You are losing the thread of what you're saying. If you don't wish to buy me, at all events you wish to buy my respect.'

'Not at all. I've told you I find it difficult to explain what I mean. You're very hard on me. Don't be angry at my chattering. You know why you ought not to be angry with me – I'm just a fool. However, I don't mind if you *are* angry. Sitting in my room, I need only think of you, I need only imagine the rustle of your dress, and at once I'm ready to chew my hands. Why should you be angry with me? Because I call myself your slave? Revel, I beg of you, in my slavery, yes, revel in it. Do you know that sometimes I could kill you? Not because I don't love you, or am jealous of you, but because I feel I want to eat you . . . Oh, now you're laughing!'

'No, I'm not!' she retorted. 'Hold your tongue, and that's an order.'

She stopped, nearly breathless with anger. God knows, she may not have been a beautiful woman, but I loved to look at her when she was brought to a halt like this, and was therefore all the more fond of arousing her temper. Perhaps she guessed this was so, and for that very reason gave way to rage. I said as much to her.

'What rubbish!' she cried with revulsion.

'I don't care,' I continued. 'And what's more, do you know that it's not safe for us to go for walks together? I often have a feeling that I want to hit you, to disfigure you, to strangle you. Are you sure it will never come to that? You're driving me crazy. Am I afraid of a scandal, or of your anger? Why should I fear your anger? I love without hope, and know that after this I will love you a thousand times more. If ever I should kill you, I would have to kill myself too. But I'll put off doing so as long as possible, because I wish to continue enjoying the unbearable pain which your coldness causes me. Do you know something very strange? It's that, with every day that passes, my love for you increases, though that would seem to be almost an impossibility. Why then should I not become a fatalist? Remember how, on the third day we climbed the Schlangenberg, I was moved to whisper in your ear: "Say but the word, and I will leap into the abyss." Had you asked me to, I would have leapt. Don't you believe me?'

'What stupid rubbish!' she exclaimed.

'I don't care whether it's wise or stupid,' I exclaimed in return. 'I only know that in your presence, I have to talk, talk, talk. So I talk. I lose all control when I'm with you, and everything ceases to matter.'

'Why would I have wanted you to jump off the Schlangenberg?' she said drily, and (I think) with wilful offensiveness. '*That* would have been totally useless to me.'

'That's excellent!' I exclaimed. 'I know you must have used the word "useless" to crush me. I can see through you. "Useless", did you say? Why, to give pleasure is *always* of some use; and, as for barbarous, unlimited power – even if it is only over a fly – why, it's a kind of luxury. People are despots by nature, and love to torture other creatures. You, in particular, love to do so.'

I remember that at this moment she looked at me in a peculiar way. The fact is, my face must have been expressing the whole tangle of senseless, gross sensations that were seething within me. To this day I can remember the conversation word for word, just as I have written it down. My eyes were suffused with blood, and my lips were caked with foam. Moreover, I swear on my honour that, had she asked me to throw myself from the summit of the Schlangenberg, I would have done it. Yes, whether she had asked me to do so in jest, or merely in contempt to spit in my face, I would have thrown myself off.

'No! Well, why then? I believe you,' she said, but in such a manner – in the manner of which, at times, she was a mistress – and with such a note of disdain and viperish arrogance in her tone, that God knows I could have killed her. Yes, at that moment she stood in real danger. I hadn't been lying to her about that.

'Surely you aren't a coward?' she asked me suddenly.

'I don't know,' I replied. 'Perhaps I am, but I don't know. I have long given up thinking about such things.'

'If I said to you, "Kill that man", would you kill him?'

'Who?'

'Whoever I wish.'

'The Frenchman?'

'Don't ask questions, give me answers. I repeat – "whoever I wish". I want to see if you were speaking seriously just now.'

She waited for me to reply, with such gravity and impatience that I felt a bit odd.

'No,' I said, '*you* tell *me* what's going on here. Why do you seem half-afraid of me? I can see for myself what's wrong. You're the step-daughter of a ruined and crazy man who is smitten with love for this devil of a Blanche. And there is this Frenchman, too, with his mysterious influence over you. Yet you actually ask me such a question! If you don't tell me how things stand, I will go mad and do something foolish. Are you ashamed to be frank with me? Are you shy of me?'

'I'm not going to talk to you about that. I've asked you a question, and I'm waiting for an answer.'

'All right, then, I *will* kill whoever you wish,' I said. 'But are you really going to ask me to do something like that?'

'Why would you think I'm going to let you off with it? I will tell you to either do it or renounce me. Could you ever do that? No, you know you couldn't. You would first kill whoever it was I asked you to kill, and then kill *me* for having dared to make you do it!'

Something seemed to strike my brain as I heard these words. Of course, at the time I took them half in jest and half as a challenge; yet she had spoken them with great seriousness. I felt thunderstruck that she should express herself like that, that she should assert such a right over me, that she should assume such authority and say outright: "Either you kill whoever I ask you to, or I'll have nothing more to do with you." Indeed, in what she had said there was something so blunt and cynical as to pass all bounds. For how could she ever look at me in the same way again after the killing was over? This was beyond slavery and abasement. Looking at someone like that raises him to your own level. Yet, despite the outrageous improbability of our conversation, my heart was trembling.

Suddenly, she burst out laughing. We were seated on a bench near the spot where the children were playing – just opposite the point in the avenue in front of the casino where the carriages draw up to set down their occupants.

'Do you see that fat Baroness?' she exclaimed. 'That's the Baroness Burmerhelm. She arrived three days ago. Just look at her husband – that tall, wizened Prussian there with the stick in his hand. Do you remember how he stared at us the other day? Well, go up to the Baroness, take off your hat to her and say something to her in French.'

'Why?'

'Because you have sworn that you would jump from the Schlangenberg for my sake, or that you would kill anyone I might ask you to kill. Well, instead of such tragedies or murders like that, all I want is a good laugh. On you go, don't argue, and let me see the Baron give you a good thrashing with his stick.'

'So you're giving me a challenge? Do you think I won't do it?'

'Yes, I'm challenging you. Off you go, that's what I want you to do.'

'Then I *will* go, no matter how mad your idea is. Only, look here: will you not be doing the General a great disservice, as well as, through him, a great disservice to yourself? It's not myself I'm worrying about, it's you and the General. Why, for a mere fancy, should I go and insult a woman?'

'Ah! I can see, then, that you're nothing but a trifler,' she said contemptuously. 'Your eyes may be bloodshot, but only because you've drunk a bit too much at dinner. Don't I know that what I've asked you to do is foolish and wrong, and that the General will be angry when he hears about it? But I want to have a good laugh all the same. That's what I want, and nothing else. Why indeed should you insult a woman? Well, you'll be given a sound thrashing for doing so.'

I turned away, and silently went off to do her bidding. Of course the thing was crazy, but I couldn't get out of it. I remember that, as I approached the Baroness, I felt as excited as a schoolboy playing a prank. I was in a bit of a frenzy, as if I was drunk.

VI

Two days have passed since that day of madness. What a noise and fuss and chatter and uproar there was! And what a welter of unseemliness and disorder and stupidity and bad manners it all was! And I was the cause of it all! Yet part of the scene was also ridiculous – at all events it seemed so to me. I'm not quite sure what was the matter with me – whether I was slightly mad or whether I deliberately kicked over the traces and ran amok. At times my mind seems all confused, while at other times I seem almost to be back in my childhood, at my school desk, and to have done the deed simply out of mischief.

It was all Polina's doing – yes, Polina's. But for her, there might never have been a fracas. Or did I perhaps do the deed in a fit of despair (however foolish it may be for me to think so)? What there is that is so attractive about her I cannot think. Yet there *is* something attractive about her – something really attractive, or so it seems to me. There are others besides myself that she has driven to distraction. She is tall and straight and very slim. Her body looks as though it could be tied in a knot or bent double like a rope. The shape of her foot is long and narrow. It torments you – yes, torments you! And her hair has a reddish tint about it, and her eyes are like cat's eyes – and able to look at you proudly and disdainfully. On the evening of my first arrival, four months ago, I remember she was sitting conversing animatedly with De Griers in the salon. And the way she looked at him was such that later on, when I retired to my own room upstairs, I kept fancying that she'd slapped him in the face – that she had slapped him right on the cheek and then stood looking at him. I've been in love with her ever since that evening.

But to my tale.

I stepped off the path on to the carriageway, and took my stance in the middle of it. And there I waited for the Baron and the Baroness. When they were but a few paces away from me, I took off my hat and bowed.

I remember that the Baroness was clad in a voluminous silk dress, pale grey in colour, and adorned with flounces and a crinoline and train. Also, she was short and inordinately fat, while her gross, flabby chin completely concealed her neck. Her face was purple, and the little eyes in it had an impudent, malicious expression. Yet she walked as though she were conferring a favour on everybody by doing so. As for the Baron, he was tall, wizened and, like most Germans, wry-faced, and he was wearing spectacles. He would be about forty-five. And he had legs that seemed to begin almost at his chest – a sign of good breeding! Yet, for all his air of peacock-like conceit, his clothes were a little baggy, and he had a sheep-like look on his face which some might have taken for a look of profundity.

These details I noted within the space of a few seconds.

At first my bow and the fact that I had my hat in my hand barely caught their attention. The Baron only scowled a little, and the Baroness swept straight on.

'Madame la Baronne,' said I, loudly and distinctly – embroidering each word, as it were – 'j'ai l'honneur d'être votre esclave.'[11]

Then I bowed again, put on my hat, and walked past the Baron with a polite smile on my face.

Polina had ordered me merely to take off my hat: the bow and the general effrontery were my own invention. God knows what led me to perpetrate such an outrage! In my madness, I felt like I was walking on air.

'Hein?' exclaimed – or rather, growled – the Baron as he turned towards me in angry surprise.

I turned as well, and stood waiting in respectful expectation. Yet I still had an impudent smile on my face as I looked at him. He seemed to hesitate, and raised his eyebrows as far as they would go. His face was growing darker by the second. The Baroness also turned in my direction, and gazed at me in anger and confusion, while some of the passers-by also began to stare at us, and others stopped in their tracks.

'Hein?' said the Baron again, with an even louder growl and a note of growing wrath in his voice.

'Ja wohl!'[12] I replied, still looking him straight in the eyes.

'Sind Sie rasend?'[13] he exclaimed, brandishing his stick, and, apparently, beginning to feel nervous. Perhaps it was my clothes that intimidated him, because I was well and fashionably dressed, in the manner of a man who belongs to indisputably good society.

'Ja wo-o-ohl!' I shouted again as loud as I could, with a long-drawnout '-ohl' in the way it is said by Berliners (who constantly use the phrase 'Ja wohl!' in conversation, and prolong the '-ohl' to a greater or lesser extent to express different shades of meaning or mood).

At this the Baron and the Baroness quickly turned round and virtually fled in their alarm. Some of the bystanders were talking excitedly and others were just staring at me in astonishment. But I don't remember the details very well.

I turned round and walked back towards Polina Alexandrovna. But when I got to within a hundred yards of where she was sitting, I saw her get up and set off towards the hotel with the children.

I caught up to her at the front entrance.

'I have performed that – that piece of stupidity,' I said as I came up to her.

'Have you? Then you can take the consequences,' she replied without so much as looking at me. Then she walked towards the staircase.

I spent the rest of the evening walking in the park. From there I went into the forest, and walked on until I even found myself in the neighbouring principality. At a wayside restaurant, I ate an omelette and drank some wine, and for which idyllic repast I was charged a thaler and a half.

I didn't return home till eleven o'clock – when I found a summons awaiting me from the General.

Our party occupies two suites in the hotel, comprising four rooms. The first (the larger one) is the drawing-room, with a grand piano, and adjoining it another large room, the General's study. It was here that he was waiting for me, standing posed in a majestic attitude beside his writing-table. De Griers was there too, sprawled on the divan.

'My good sir,' the General began, 'may I ask you what you think you have gone and done?'

'I would be glad,' I replied, 'if we could come straight to the point. Probably you are referring to my encounter today with a certain German?'

'With a certain German? Why, that German was the Baron Burmerhelm, a most important person! I hear you have been rude both to him and to the Baroness.'

'No, I have not.'

'But I understand that you simply terrified them, my good sir,' shouted the General.

'Not in the least,' I replied. 'When I was in Berlin, I frequently heard the Berliners repeat, and prolong to a revolting length, a certain word – namely, this "Jawohl!" And happening to meet this couple in the carriage-drive, I found, for some reason or another, that this word suddenly came back to my mind, and really irritated me. Moreover, on the three previous occasions that I have met the Baroness, she has walked towards me as though I were a worm which could easily be crushed underfoot. Not unnaturally, I too have some self-respect, so on *this* occasion I took off my hat and said politely (yes, I assure you it was said politely): 'Madame, j'ai l'honneur d'être votre esclave.' Then the Baron turned round, and said 'Hein?', whereupon I felt moved to shout out in reply 'Jawohl!' I shouted it at him twice – the first time in an ordinary tone of voice, and the second time drawling out the word as much as I could. And that's all.'

I must confess that this puerile explanation gave me great pleasure. I was feeling a strong desire to make the story as absurd as possible. And so the more I talked, the more I relished my telling of the tale.

'You're just making fun of me!' shouted the General as, turning to the Frenchman, he declared in French that I had just done it to make trouble. De Griers smiled contemptuously, and shrugged his shoulders.

'Do not think *that*,' I put in. 'It was not like that at all. I grant you that my behaviour was bad – I fully confess that it was so, and make no secret of the fact. I would even go so far as to grant you that my behaviour might well be called a stupid and improper piece of tomfoolery; but *more* than that it was not. Also, let me tell you that I am very sorry for my conduct. Yet there is one circumstance which, in my eyes, almost absolves me from regret in the matter. Of late – that is to say, for the last two or three weeks – I have been feeling not at all well. That is to say, I have been in a sick, nervous, irritable, capricious condition, to the extent that I have at times lost control over myself. For instance, on more than one occasion I have tried to pick a quarrel even with Monsieur le Marquis here; but let's not go into that, it might offend him. In short, I have recently been showing signs of ill-health. Whether the Baroness Burmerhelm will take this into consideration when I beg her forgiveness (for I do intend to ask her forgiveness), I do not know; but I doubt if she will, and all the less so since, I know, the excuse is one which, of late, has begun to be abused in the legal world, in that advocates in criminal cases have taken to justifying their clients on the grounds that, at the moment of committing the crime, they (the clients) were not aware of what they were doing – that, in short, they were out of sorts. "My client committed the murder, that is true, but he has no recollection of having committed it." And doctors actually support these advocates by affirming that there really is such an illness, that there really can arise temporary delusions which make a man remember nothing of a given deed, or only half or a quarter of it! But the Baron and Baroness belong to an older generation, as well as being Prussian nobility and landowners. To them such an advance in the medico-judicial world will be quite unknown, and therefore they are all the more unlikely to accept any such explanation. What do *you* think, General?'

'Enough, sir!' he thundered, with barely restrained fury. 'That's enough, I say! Once and for all, I am going to rid myself of you and your impertinence. On no account are you to try to apologise to the Baron and Baroness. Any communication with you, even confined to your begging their pardon, they would look upon as beneath them. I may tell you that, on learning that you belonged to my household, the

Baron approached me in the casino and almost demanded satisfaction of me. Do you understand, then, what it is you have brought upon me – upon *me*, my good sir? You have made me apologise humbly to the Baron and give him my word of honour that this very day you will cease to belong to my establishment!'

'Excuse me, General,' I interrupted, 'but did he make an express point of it that I should "cease to belong to your establishment", as you put it?'

'No, I thought, on my own initiative, that I ought to give him that satisfaction. And he was satisfied with it. So we must part, my good sir. I owe you forty-three gulden, as per the accompanying statement. Here's the money, and here's the account, which you are at liberty to check. Goodbye. From this time on, we are strangers. I have never had anything but trouble and unpleasantness from you. I'm just about to call the manager to explain to him that from tomorrow onwards I shall no longer be responsible for your hotel expenses. I have the honour to remain your obedient servant.'

I took the money and the account (which was written in pencil) and, bowing low to the General, said to him very gravely:

'The matter cannot end here. I regret very much that you should have been put to any unpleasantness at the Baron's hands, but the fault (if you will pardon me) is your own. How is it that you took it upon yourself to answer for me to the Baron? And what did you mean by saying that I was part of your household? I'm merely your family tutor, not your son, nor your ward, nor a person of any kind for whose acts you need be responsible. I am a judicially competent person, a man of twenty-five years of age, a university graduate, a gentleman and, until I met you, a complete stranger to you. Only my boundless respect for your merits restrains me from demanding satisfaction at your hands, as well as a further explanation as to the reasons which led you to take it upon yourself to answer for my conduct.'

So struck was he with my words that, spreading out his hands, he turned to the Frenchman and informed him that I had almost challenged him (the General) to a duel. The Frenchman laughed out loud.

'Nor do I intend to let the Baron off,' I continued calmly, but with not a little discomfiture at De Griers' amusement. 'And since you, General, have today been so good as to listen to the Baron's complaints and to side with him – since, I say, you have made yourself a party to the affair – I have the honour to inform you that, tomorrow morning at the latest, I shall, in my own name, demand of the said Baron a formal explanation as to why he disregarded the fact that this matter is between him and myself alone and slighted me by referring it to another person as though I were unworthy to answer for my own conduct.'

What happened next was what I had expected. The General, on hearing of this further intended outrage, lost his nerve.

'What?' he cried. 'Do you intend to go on with this damned nonsense? Do you not realise the harm it is doing me? Don't you dare, sir, don't you dare! We have police authorities here who, out of respect for my rank and the Baron's would . . . In short, sir, I swear I'll have you arrested and marched out of town to prevent any further disturbance on your part. Do you understand?' He was almost breathless with anger, as well as in a terrible fright.

'General,' I replied with that calmness he never could abide, 'one cannot arrest a man for disturbing the peace until he has disturbed the peace. I have not so much as begun my explanations to the Baron, and you are totally ignorant about how and when I intend to do so. I only wish to disabuse the Baron of what is, to me, a shameful supposition – namely, that I am under the guardianship of some person who is qualified to exercise control over my free will. There is no need for you to worry yourself.'

'For God's sake, Alexei Ivanovich, do put an end to this senseless scheme of yours!' he muttered, but with a sudden change from a truculent tone to one of entreaty as he grasped my hand. 'Do you know what is likely to come of it? Further unpleasantness, that's all. You will agree with me, I'm sure, that at present I have to behave with particular care – yes, especially now, especially at the moment. You don't fully realise my position. When we leave this place, I'll be ready to receive you back into my household, but for the time being, I – well, you know my reasons.' With that he wound up in a despairing voice: 'Oh, Alexei Ivanovich, Alexei Ivanovich!'

I moved towards the door, begging him to be calm and promising that everything would be done decently and in order. Then I left.

Russians, when abroad, have a tendency to be too timid, to watch all their words, and to wonder what people are thinking of their conduct or whether this or that is "the done thing". In short, they are apt to behave too rigidly, especially those who lay claim to great importance. They always prefer the form of behaviour which is already accepted and established. This they will follow slavishly, whether in hotels, on promenades, at meetings or when on a journey. But the General had admitted to me that, over and above such considerations as these, there were circumstances which compelled him to "move with especial care at present", and that this fact had actually made him mean-spirited and a coward, to completely change his tone towards me. This fact I duly noted and took into my calculations, because, of course, he *might* apply to the authorities tomorrow, and it would be wise for me to tread carefully.

Yet it was not the General but Polina that I wanted to make angry. She had treated me with such cruelty, and had got me into such a hole, that I was longing to make her beg me to stop. Of course, my foolish prank might compromise her. But apart from that, certain other feelings and desires had begun to form themselves in my brain. Even if I were never to amount in her eyes to anything more than a nonentity, that didn't mean that other people would look on me as a namby-pamby nobody, and the Baron certainly wasn't going to give me a thrashing; but the fact was that I wanted to have the last laugh over them all and for myself to come out of this unscathed. Just let people watch. Let Polina, for once, get a real fright, and be forced to whistle me to heel again. But, however much she might whistle, she would see that I was at least not a weakling and a nobody!

I have just received a surprising piece of news. I have just met our nanny on the stairs and been informed by her that Maria Philippovna left today, by the night train, to stay with a cousin in Karlsbad. What can that mean? Nanny says that she has been meaning to go for some time, but how is it that no one else seems to have been aware of that? Or have I been the only person to be unaware of it? Also, Nanny has just told me that, three days ago, Maria Philippovna had words with the General. That I understand! They were probably arguing about Mademoiselle Blanche. Yes, there's definitely something decisive in the offing.

VII

In the morning I sent for the maître d'hôtel, and explained to him that, in future, my bill was to be given to me personally. As a matter of fact, my expenses had never been so large as to alarm me, nor to force me to leave the hotel; moreover, I still had a hundred and sixty gulden left, and in them – yes, in them – riches perhaps awaited me. It was a curious fact, that, although I had not yet won anything by gambling, I was nevertheless behaving, thinking and feeling as if I was wealthy. I couldn't imagine myself otherwise.

Despite the earliness of the hour, I had decided to go and see Mr Astley, who was staying at the Hôtel de l'Angleterre (a hostelry at no great distance from our own). But suddenly De Griers appeared. This had never before happened, for of late that gentleman and I had been on the most strained and distant terms – he making no attempt to conceal his contempt for me (he even made an express point of showing it) and I having no reason to desire his company. In short, I detested him. Consequently, his coming to see me astounded me all the more. I at once guessed that something out of the ordinary was brewing.

He came in with marked affability, and began by complimenting me on my room. Then, noticing that I had my hat in my hands, he inquired where I was going so early; and learning that I was going to see Mr Astley on a matter of business, he stopped, looked grave and seemed deep in thought.

He was a true Frenchman insofar as that, though he could be lively and engaging when it suited him, he became insufferably dull and wearisome as soon as the need for being lively and engaging had passed. Seldom is a Frenchman *naturally* polite: he is polite only to order and for a purpose. For example, if he thinks it incumbent on him to be whimsical, original and unconventional, his behaviour is always silly and unnatural because it consists of trite and hackneyed forms. In short, the natural Frenchman is a conglomeration of common-place, petty, everyday sobriety, making him the most tedious person in the world. Indeed, I believe that only the innocent and inexperienced, especially Russians, feel an attraction towards the French; for, to any man of sensibility, such a compendium of outworn forms, of drawing-room manners, familiarity and gaiety, becomes instantly noticeable and quite unbearable.

'I have come to see you on business,' De Griers began, in a very aloof but polite tone, 'and I will not conceal from you the fact that I have come as an emissary, or rather as an intermediary, from the General. Having little knowledge of Russian, I missed most of what was said last night, but the General has now explained matters to me, and I must confess that—'

'Look here, Monsieur de Griers,' I interrupted. 'I understand that you have undertaken to act in this affair as an intermediary. Of course I'm only an "utchitel", a tutor, and have never claimed to be an intimate of this household or to stand on anything like familiar terms with it. Consequently, I don't know the whole of its circumstances. Yet pray explain to me this: have you yourself become one of its members, seeing that you are beginning to take such a part in everything, and are now here as an intermediary?'

The Frenchman seemed displeased at my question. It was too outspoken for his taste, and he was in no mind to be frank with me.

'I am connected with the General,' he said drily, 'partly through business affairs, and partly through special circumstances. My principal has sent me merely to ask you to forego your intentions of yesterday evening. What you contemplate is, I have no doubt, very clever but he has charged me to represent to you that you have not the slightest chance of succeeding in your intention, since not only will the Baron refuse to receive you but he also has at his disposal every possible means for obviating further unpleasantness from you. Surely you can see that yourself? What, then, would be the good of going on with it all? On the other hand, the General promises that at the first favourable opportunity he will receive you back into his household, and, in the meantime, will credit you with your salary, with "vos appointements". Surely that is to your advantage, is it not?'

Very quietly, I replied that he (the Frenchman) was labouring under a delusion; that perhaps, after all, I would not be expelled from the Baron's presence but, on the contrary, be listened to; and finally, that I would be glad if Monsieur de Griers would admit that he was now visiting me merely to see how far I intended to go in the affair.

'Good heavens!' exclaimed De Griers. 'Seeing that the General has such an interest in the matter, is there anything so unnatural in his desire to know what you are planning to do?'

I began to explain, and he listened, sprawled out with his head inclined to one side in my direction and with an expression of open and unconcealed irony on his face. In short, he adopted a supercilious attitude towards me. For my own part, I endeavoured to pretend that I took the affair very seriously. I declared that, since the Baron had gone and complained about me to the General, as though I were a mere servant of the General's, he had, in the first place, lost me my post, and, in the second place, treated me like a person who, as to one not qualified to answer for himself, it was not even worthwhile speaking to. Naturally, I said, I felt insulted at this. Yet, understanding as I did our differences in age, in social status and so on (here I could scarcely help smiling), I was not anxious to bring about further scenes by going personally to demand or request satisfaction from the Baron. All I felt was that I had a right to go in person and beg the Baron's and the Baroness's pardon – the more so since, of late, I had been feeling unwell and out of sorts and had been in a mischievous frame of mind. And so on, and so forth. But, I continued, the Baron's offensive behaviour to me yesterday (that is to say, the fact of his referring the matter to the General) as well as his insistence that the General should deprive me of my post, had placed me in such a position that I could not well express my regret to him (the Baron) and to his good lady, for the reason that in all probability both he and the Baroness, with the world at large, would imagine that I was doing so merely because I hoped, by my action, to recover my post. Hence, I found myself forced to request that the Baron express to me *his own* regrets, and in the most unqualified manner – to say, in fact, that he had never had any wish to insult me. After the Baron had done *that*, I would, for my part, at once feel free to express to him, whole-heartedly and without reserve, my own regrets. 'In short,' I declared in conclusion, 'my one desire is that the Baron may make it possible for me to adopt the latter course.'

'Oh, for goodness sake! What refinement and punctiliousness!' exclaimed De Griers. 'Besides, what have you got to express regret for? Admit it, Monsieur . . . Monsieur . . . pardon me . . . Alexei, isn't it? . . . but I've forgotten your surname – admit, I say, that all this is merely a plan to annoy the General. Or perhaps you have some other and special purpose in mind? Eh?'

'In return you must pardon *me*, my dear Marquis, and tell me what it has to do with you.'

'The General—0'

'What about the General? Last night he said that, for some reason or another, it behoved him to "move with especial care at present". So he was feeling nervous about something, but I didn't understand what.'

'Yes, there *do* exist special reasons for his feeling so,' agreed De Griers in a conciliatory tone, yet with mounting irritation. 'You are acquainted with Mademoiselle de Cominges, are you not?'

'Mademoiselle Blanche, you mean?'

'Yes, Mademoiselle Blanche de Cominges, and Madame her mother. Doubtless you know that the General is in love with this young lady, and may even be about to marry her before he leaves here? Imagine, therefore, what any scene or scandal would do to him!'

'I can't see any scene or scandals affecting the marriage plans.'

'Mais le Baron est si irascible – un caractère prussien, vous savez! Enfin il fera une querelle d'Allemand.'[14]

'With me, then, but not with you,' I replied, 'seeing that I no longer belong to the household.' (I was deliberately trying to talk as foolishly as possible.) 'But is it quite settled that Mademoiselle Blanche is to marry the General? What are they waiting for? Why should they conceal such a matter – at all events from us, the General's own people?'

'I can't say. The marriage is not yet a settled affair, because they are waiting for news from Russia. The General has business affairs to settle.'

'Ah! Something, no doubt, to do with "Granny"?'

De Griers glanced at me with a look of hatred.

'To cut things short,' he interrupted, 'I have complete confidence in your native courtesy, as well as in your tact and good sense. I feel sure you will do what I suggest, even if only for the sake of this family which has received you like a kinsman into its bosom and has always loved and respected you.'

'Be so good as to observe,' I remarked, 'that this same family has just *expelled* me from its bosom. Now you're saying that it was only done for show. But when people have just said to you, "Of course we don't wish to throw you out, but for the sake of appearances you must allow yourself to be thrown out", it amounts pretty much to the same thing.'

'Very well, then,' he said, in a sterner and more arrogant tone. 'Seeing that my solicitations have had no effect upon you, it is my duty to tell you that other measures will be taken. Remember, there are police here, and they'll send you packing this very day. Que diable![15] To think of a blanc-bec[16] like yourself challenging a person like the Baron to a duel! Do you suppose that you will be *allowed* to do such things? Just try it, and see if anyone is afraid of you! The reason why I have asked you to desist is that I can see that your conduct is irritating the General. And do you really think the Baron couldn't just tell his man to throw you out?'

'But I wouldn't *go* out,' I retorted, with absolute calmness. 'You are labouring under a delusion, Monsieur de Griers. The thing will be done with far greater refinement than you imagine. I was just about to start for Mr Astley's, to ask him to be my intermediary – in other words, my second. He likes me, and I don't think he'll refuse. He will go and see the Baron on my behalf, and the Baron will certainly not refuse to receive him. Although I am only a tutor, a kind of "subaltern", Mr Astley is known to all men as the nephew of a real lord, Lord Piebrock, and that lord is here. Yes, you may be pretty sure that the Baron will be civil to Mr Astley, and listen to him. On the other hand, should he decline to do so, Mr Astley will take the refusal as a personal affront to himself (you know how the English are) and thereupon introduce to the Baron a friend of his own (and he has many friends of rank). That being so, picture to yourself the outcome of the affair, an affair which will not quite end as you think it will.'

This caused the Frenchman to lose his nerve. 'Things may really be as this fellow says,' he was evidently thinking. 'He might *really* be able to engineer another scenario.'

'Once more I beg of you to let the matter drop,' he continued, in a tone that was now entirely conciliatory. 'One would think that it actually *pleased* you to cause scenes! Indeed, it's a brawl rather than genuine satisfaction that you're looking for. I have said that the affair may prove to be diverting, and even clever, and that possibly you may attain something by it, but nonetheless I tell you' (he said this only because he saw me rise and reach for my hat) 'that I have come here also to hand you these few words from a certain person. Read them now, please, because I must take her back an answer.'

So saying, he took from his pocket a small, compact, wafer-sealed note, and handed it to me. In Polina's handwriting, I read:

'I hear that you are thinking of going on with this affair. You have lost your temper now, and are beginning to play the fool! But there are special circumstances here that I may explain to you later on. Pray stop this folly and control yourself. For folly it all is. I need you, and, moreover, you have promised to obey me. Remember the Schlangenberg. I am asking you to be obedient. If necessary, I will even *order* you to be obedient. – Your own P.

'P.S. If you still bear a grudge against me for what happened last night, please forgive me.'

Everything, to my eyes, seemed to change as I read these words. My lips grew pale, and I began to tremble. Meanwhile, that damn Frenchman was watching me with a pretence of discretion, as though he wished to avoid witnessing my confusion. It would have been better if he had just laughed outright.

'Very well,' I said, 'you can tell Mademoiselle not to worry herself.

But,' I added sharply, 'I would also ask you why you have been so long in handing me this note? Instead of chattering about trifles, you ought to have handed me the missive at once, if you really were commissioned as you say you were.'

'Well, pardon some natural impatience on my part, for this situation is so bizarre. I first wanted to get some personal knowledge of your intentions, and, moreover, I didn't know the contents of the note and thought that it could be given you at any time.'

'I understand,' I replied. 'So you were ordered to hand me the note only as a last resort, if you could not otherwise convince me? Is it not so? Admit it, Monsieur de Griers.'

'Perhaps,' said he, assuming a look of great forbearance, but gazing at me in a meaningful way.

I reached for my hat, at which he nodded and left. But on his lips I fancied I could see a mocking smile. How could it have been otherwise?

'You and I will settle things between us later, Mister Frenchman,' I muttered as I went down the stairs. 'Yes, we will, you and I.' But my thoughts were all in confusion, as if something had knocked me senseless. Presently the air revived me a little, and, a couple of minutes later, my brain had sufficiently cleared to allow two ideas in particular to stand out. Firstly, I asked myself, which of the absurd, extravagant, schoolboyish threats I had uttered at random last night had made everybody so alarmed? Secondly, what was the influence this Frenchman had over Polina? He had but to say the word and at once she did what he wanted, writing me a note to beg me to desist! Of course, the relations between the pair had, from the very beginning, been a riddle to me; they had been so ever since I had first made their acquaintance. But of late I had noticed in her a strong aversion towards him, even a contempt for him, while, for his part, he scarcely even looked at her, but always behaved towards her in the most churlish manner. Yes, I had noticed all that. What's more, Polina herself had mentioned to me her dislike of him; she had made some remarkable confessions on the subject. Hence, he must have got her into his power somehow, holding her in a vice-like grip.

VIII

I came face to face with my Englishman on the promenade, as it was called, that is to say, in the chestnut avenue.

'Oh, I was just coming to see you,' he said, catching sight of me, 'and you appear to be out on a similar errand. So you've parted company with your employers?'

'How do you know that?' I asked in astonishment. 'Does *everyone* know that?'

'By no means. Not everyone would consider such a fact to be of any importance. Indeed, I've never heard anyone speak of it.'

'Then how is it that you know?'

'Because I happen to have found out. Where will you go? I like you, so I was coming to pay you a visit.'

'What a splendid fellow you are, Mr Astley!' I exclaimed, though still wondering how he had come by his knowledge. 'And since I have not yet had my coffee, and you have, in all probability, scarcely touched yours, let's adjourn to the casino café where we can sit and smoke and have a talk.'

The café in question was only a hundred yards away. When the coffee had been brought, we sat down, and I lit a cigarette. Astley was no smoker, but, taking a seat by my side, he settled down to listen.

'I don't intend to go away,' was the first thing I said. 'I intend, on the contrary, to remain here.'

'That I never doubted,' he answered good-humouredly.

It is a curious fact that, on my way to see him, I had never even thought of telling him of my love for Polina. In fact, I had meant to avoid any mention of the subject. During our stay in the place, I had hardly ever said a word about it. You see, not only was Astley a very shy man, but also I had perceived from the first that Polina had made a great impression on him, although he never spoke about her. But now, strangely enough, he had no sooner seated himself and fixed his steely gaze on me, than, for some reason or another, I felt moved to tell him everything, to speak to him of my love in all its aspects. I spoke on the subject for an hour and a half, and found it a pleasure to do so, even though this was the first occasion on which I had referred to the matter. Indeed, when, at certain moments, I could see that my more ardent utterances embarrassed him, I deliberately increased the ardour of my tale. Yet one thing I regret: and that is that I may have said too much about the Frenchman . . .

Mr Astley listened to me, motionless. Not a word nor a sound of any kind did he utter as he stared into my eyes. Suddenly, however, on my mentioning the Frenchman, he interrupted me, and inquired sternly whether I was right to speak of this irrelevant matter. (He had always had a strange way of phrasing his questions.)

'No, I fear you're right, I have no right to do so,' I replied.

'And concerning this Marquis and Miss Polina, is it not the case that you know nothing beyond conjecture?'

Again I was surprised that such a straight question should come from such a shy individual.

'No, I know nothing *for certain* about them,' was my reply. 'No, nothing.'

'Then you have done very wrong to speak of them to me, or even to imagine such things about them.'

'Quite so, quite so,' I interrupted in some astonishment. 'I admit that. But that's not the point.' Whereupon I related to him in detail what had happened yesterday. I described Polina's outburst, my encounter with the Baron, my dismissal, the General's extraordinary cowardice, and De Griers' visit that morning. Finally, I showed Astley the note.

'What do you make of it?' I asked. 'When I met you, I was just coming to ask you your opinion. For myself, I could kill this Frenchman, and perhaps I'll do so yet.'

'Me too,' said Mr Astley. 'As for Miss Polina – well, you yourself know that, if necessity forces you to, you may enter into a relationship with people you simply detest. Even between this couple there may be something which, though not known to you, depends on extraneous circumstances. I think you may reassure yourself, at all events partially. And as for Miss Polina's behaviour yesterday, it was, of course, strange, not because she can have meant to get rid of you or get you a thrashing from the Baron's stick (which for some curious reason he did not use, though he had it in his hand), but because such proceedings on the part of such a . . . well, of such a refined lady as Miss Polina, are, to say the least, unbecoming. But she can't have realised that you would carry out her absurd request to the letter.'

'Do you know what?' I exclaimed suddenly, as I fixed Mr Astley with my gaze. 'I think you've already heard the story from someone – very possibly from Miss Polina herself.'

He looked at me in astonishment.

'Your eyes are flashing,' he said, regaining his composure, 'and I can read suspicion in them. Well, you have no right whatever to be suspicious. It's not a right I acknowledge, and I absolutely refuse to answer your question.'

'That's enough! You need say no more,' I shouted with a strange emotion in my heart, not altogether understanding what had caused the thought to come into my head. Indeed, when, where, how could Polina have chosen Astley to be one of her confidants? Of late I had been paying little attention to him, and Polina had always been a riddle to me, so much so that now, when I had just allowed myself to tell my friend of my infatuation in all its facets, I was struck, during the very telling, by the fact that I could say nothing explicit, nothing positive, about my relationship with her. On the contrary, our relations had been fantastical, strange and unreal; they had been unlike anything else I could think of.

'Very well, then, very well,' I replied, gasping as if breathless. 'I'm confused, and there's a lot I don't understand. But you're a good fellow, and there's another matter I'd be glad to have your opinion about, even if not your advice.'

Then, after a pause, I continued:

'For instance, what reason do you think the General has for taking fright in this way? Why should everyone have been led to exaggerate

my stupid clowning into a serious incident? Even De Griers has found
it necessary to stick his oar in (and he only interferes on the most
important occasions), and to visit me to make the most earnest suppli-
cations. Yes, *he*, De Griers, was actually begging *me* not to do something! And, mark you, although he came to me as early as nine o'clock
in the morning, he had Miss Polina's note with him. When, I ask you,
was that note written? Miss Polina must have been aroused from sleep
for the express purpose of writing it. At all events, the circumstance
shows that she is an absolute slave to the Frenchman, since she actually begs my pardon in the note – actually begs my pardon! Yet what
is her personal concern in the matter? Why is she interested in it at
all? Why, too, is the whole party so afraid of this precious Baron? And
what are we to make of the General planning to marry Mademoiselle
Blanche de Cominges? He told me last night that, because of the
circumstances, he must "move with especial care at present". What is
your opinion of it all? From the way you're looking at me, I'm
convinced you know more about it than I do.'

Mr Astley smiled and nodded.

'Yes, I think I *do* know more about it than you do,' he agreed. 'The
whole thing concerns Mademoiselle Blanche. Of that I am certain.'

'And what about Mademoiselle Blanche, then?' I exclaimed
impatiently (for there had arisen in me a sudden hope that this would
enable me to discover something about Polina).

'Well, my belief is that at the present moment Mademoiselle Blanche
definitely has a special reason for wishing to avoid any trouble with
the Baron and Baroness. It might lead not only to some unpleasantness,
but even to a scandal.'

'Oh! Well, there's something!'

'More than that, I can tell you that Mademoiselle Blanche has been
in Roulettenburg before, because she was staying here three seasons
ago. I myself was here at the time, and in those days Mademoiselle
Blanche was not known as Mademoiselle de Cominges, nor did her
mother, the supposed Widow de Cominges, even exist. At least, no
one ever mentioned her. De Griers, too, had not materialised, and I

am convinced that not only are the parties not related to one another, but they have also not known each other very long. Moreover, De Griers' marquisate is of recent creation. Of that I have reason to be sure, owing to a certain circumstance. Even the name De Griers itself may be taken to be a recent invention, seeing that I have a friend who once met the said 'Marquis' under a different name altogether.'

'Yet doesn't he have a good number of respectable friends?'

'Possibly. Mademoiselle Blanche may have too, but it is not three years since she received from the local police, at the instance of the Baroness, an "invitation" to leave the town. And she left.'

'But why?'

'Well, I must tell you that she first appeared here in the company of an Italian – a prince of some sort, a man who bore a historic name (Barberini[17] or something like that). The fellow was simply a mass of rings and diamonds – genuine diamonds, too – and the couple used to drive out in a splendid carriage. At first Mademoiselle Blanche played trente-et-quarante with a fair amount of success, but, later, her luck took a marked change for the worse. I distinctly remember that in a single evening she lost an enormous sum of money. But worse was to come, for one fine morning her prince disappeared – horses, carriage, the lot. And the hotel bill he left unpaid was enormous. At this Mademoiselle Zelma (the name she assumed after pretending to be Madame Barberini) was in despair. She shrieked and howled all over the hotel, and even tore her clothes in her frenzy. Also staying in the hotel was a Polish count (you know, of course, that *all* Poles are counts when they're travelling about!), and the spectacle of Mademoiselle Zelma tearing her clothes and scratching her face like a cat with her beautiful, scented fingernails made a strong impression on him. So the pair had a talk together, and, by dinner time, she was consoled. Indeed, that evening the couple entered the casino arm in arm – Mademoiselle Zelma laughing loudly, as was her custom, and more free and easy in her behaviour than she had been before. For instance, she joined the ranks of those women roulette-players who, to clear a space for themselves at the tables, just push their fellow-players aside. No doubt you have noticed them?'

'Yes, certainly.'

'Well, they're not worth any attention. To the annoyance of the respectable public, they're allowed to remain here, at least such of them as daily change 1000-franc notes at the tables (though, as soon as ever these women cease to do so, they are invited to depart). However, Mademoiselle Zelma continued to change notes of this kind, but her play grew more and more unsuccessful, despite the fact that such ladies' luck is frequently good, as they have a surprising amount of cash at their disposal. Suddenly, the Count too disappeared, just as the Prince had done, and that same evening Mademoiselle Zelma was forced to appear in the casino alone. On this occasion no one offered her his arm. Two days later she had come to the end of her funds; whereupon, after staking and losing her last louis d'or she chanced to look around her, and saw standing by her side the Baron Burmerhelm, who had been eyeing her with obvious disapproval. However, Mademoiselle paid no attention to that, but, turning to him with her well-known smile, asked him to stake, on her behalf, a hundred florins on red. Later that evening a complaint from the Baroness led the authorities to request Mademoiselle not to come back to the casino. If you feel in any way surprised that I should know these petty and unedifying details, the reason is that I had them from a relative of mine who, later that evening, drove Mademoiselle Zelma in his carriage from Roulettenburg to Spa. Now, listen: Mademoiselle wants to become Madame General, so that, in future, she may be spared receiving such invitations from casino authorities as she did three years ago. At present she's not gambling, but that's only because, it seems, she is lending money to other players. Yes, that's a much more lucrative game. I even suspect that the unfortunate General himself is in her debt, as well, perhaps, as De Griers. Or, it may be that the latter has entered into a partnership with her. Consequently you yourself will see that, until the marriage has been consummated, Mademoiselle would scarcely like to have the attention of the Baron and the Baroness drawn to herself. Quite simply, to anyone in her position a scandal would be most detrimental. You belong to the household of these people, so any action of yours might cause such a scandal – and the more so since daily she appears in public arm in arm with the General or with Miss Polina. *Now* do you understand?'

'No, I don't!' I shouted, banging my fist down upon the table – banging it with such violence that a frightened waiter came running towards us. 'Tell me, Mr Astley, why, if you knew this story all along, and, consequently, always knew who this Mademoiselle Blanche is, you never warned either myself or the General, nor, most of all, Miss Polina who is accustomed to appear in the casino, in fact everywhere in public, with Mademoiselle Blanche. How could you do it?'

'It would have done no good to warn you,' he replied quietly, 'because you could have done nothing about it. What was I to warn you against? As likely as not, the General knows more about Mademoiselle Blanche than I do, and yet the unfortunate man still walks around with her and Miss Polina. Only yesterday I saw this Frenchwoman riding, splendidly mounted, with De Griers, while the General was cantering along in their wake on a roan horse. He had said, that morning, that his legs were hurting him, but he was able to sit well enough on a saddle. As he passed, I looked at him, and the thought occurred to me that he was a man lost for ever. However, it's no business of mine, as I have just recently had the happiness to make Miss Polina's acquaintance. Anyway' – this he added as an afterthought – 'I've already told you that I do not recognise your right to ask me certain questions, no matter how sincere my liking is for you.'

'Enough,' I said, rising. 'To me it's as clear as day that Miss Polina knows all about this Mademoiselle Blanche but cannot bring herself to part with her Frenchman, so she consents also to be seen in public with Mademoiselle Blanche. You may be sure that nothing else would ever have induced her either to walk around with this Frenchwoman or to send me a note not to bother the Baron. Yes, it's *there* that the influence lies before which everything else must bow! Yet it was she herself who set me at the Baron! The devil take it, I can't make sense of this at all.'

'You forget, in the first place, that this Mademoiselle de Cominges is the General's intended, and, in the second place, that Miss Polina, the General's step-daughter, has a younger brother and sister who, though they are the General's own children, are completely neglected by this madman, and robbed by him as well.'

'Yes, yes, that's so. To desert the children now would mean their total abandonment, whereas to remain means being able to defend their interests, and, perhaps, save a portion of the estate for them. Yes, yes, that's quite true. And yet, and yet . . . Oh, I can well understand why they're all so interested in "Granny"!'

'Who?' asked Mr Astley.

'The old hag in Moscow who refuses to die, yet about whom they are constantly hoping for a telegram notifying them of her death.'

'Ah, so, of course, their interests centre on her. It is a question of succession. Let that be settled, and the General will marry, Mademoiselle Polina will be set free, and De Griers . . .'

'What about De Griers?'

'. . . will be repaid his money, which is what he is now waiting for.'

'What? Do you think that all he's waiting for?'

'I don't know any more than that,' said Mr Astley, and would say no more.

'But I do, I do!' I shouted in fury. 'He too is waiting for the old woman's will, because it awards Miss Polina a dowry. As soon as she gets the money, she will throw herself round the Frenchman's neck. All women are like that. Even the proudest of them become abject slaves where marriage is concerned. All Polina is good for is to fall head over ears in love. That's what *I* think, anyway. Look at her, especially when she's sitting alone and deep in thought. All this is pre-ordained, fated . . . and accursed. Polina is capable of any mad act of passion. She . . . she . . . but who's that calling for me?' I broke off. 'I heard someone calling in Russian "Alexei Ivanovich!" It was a woman's voice. Listen, listen!'

By then we were approaching my hotel. We had left the café long ago, almost without noticing we had done so.

'Yes, I *did* hear a woman's voice calling, but I don't know who she's calling for. It was in Russian. Ah! *Now* I can see where all the shouting is coming from. It's from that lady there, the one who's sitting on the armchair, the one who has just been escorted to the hotel door by a crowd of flunkeys. Look at that pile of luggage behind her! She must have arrived by train.'

'But why should she be calling *me*? Listen, she's calling again! Look! Now she's waving to us!'

'So she is,' agreed Mr Astley.

'Alexei Ivanovich, Alexei Ivanovich! Oh, good heavens, what a stupid fellow!' came a despairing wail from the hotel entrance.

We had almost reached the entrance, and I was just setting foot on the steps in front of it when my hands fell limply to my sides in astonishment and my feet were rooted to the spot.

IX

For there, on the top step of the hotel entrance, having been carried up the steps in an armchair, surrounded by a host of footmen, maids and other menials belonging to the hotel staff, and with the head waiter himself having actually run out to meet this visitor who had arrived with so much fuss and noise, there, attended by her own retinue and accompanied by an immense pile of trunks and suitcases was – *Grandmother*! Yes, it was her, the wealthy, imposing, seventy-five-year-old Antonida Vasilyevna Tarasevicheva, landowner and *grande dame* of Moscow, the 'Granny' who had caused so many telegrams to be sent and received, who was dying, but not dying, who had descended on us in person like snow might fall from the clouds! Though unable to walk, she had arrived carried aloft in an armchair (her mode of conveyance for the last five years), as brisk, aggressive, self-satisfied, bolt-upright, loudly imperious and generally abusive as ever. In fact, she looked exactly as she had on the only two occasions when I had seen her since my appointment to the General's household. Naturally enough, I was speechless with astonishment. She had spotted me a hundred paces away! Even while she was being carried along in her chair, she had recognised me and called me by name (which, as usual, after hearing only once, she had remembered for ever afterwards).

'And this is the woman they had thought to see dead and buried and leaving them a legacy!' I thought to myself. 'She'll outlive us all, and everyone else in the hotel. Good Lord! What's going to become of us now? What on earth will happen to the General? She'll turn the place upside down!'

'My good man,' the old woman continued, shouting at me, 'what are you doing standing there with your eyes almost popping out of your head? Can't you come and say how-do-you-do? Are you too proud to shake hands? Or don't you recognise me? Here, Potapych!' she exclaimed to an old servant with a bald, red head, dressed in a frock coat and white waistcoat (he was the chamberlain who always accompanied her on her journeys). 'Just think! Alexei Ivanovich doesn't recognise me! They really have buried me! Yes, and after sending dozens of telegrams to find out if I was dead or not! Yes, yes, I've heard the whole story. I am very much alive, though, as you can see.'

'I do beg your pardon, Antonida Vasilyevna,' I replied cheerfully, as I recovered my presence of mind. 'I have no reason to wish you ill. I'm just rather astonished to see you. Why should I not be, seeing how unexpected . . .'

'Why should you be astonished? I just got on to a train, and came. Things were quiet enough in the train, and it didn't jolt. Have you been out for a walk?'

'Yes. I've just been to the casino.'

'Oh? Well, it's quite nice here,' she went on as she looked around her. 'The place seems comfortable, and all the trees are green. I like that. Are the family at home? Is the General inside?'

'Yes, probably all of them at this time of the day.'

'So they observe set hours here too, do they, and keep up appearances? Such things always give one tone. I've heard they're keeping a carriage, just like Russian gentry ought to do. When abroad, our Russian people always cut a dash. Is Praskovya here too?'

'Yes. Polina Alexandrovna is here.'

'And that French fellow? Well, whatever, I'll go and see them myself. Alexei Ivanovich, show me the quickest way to their rooms. Do you like it here?'

'Yes, thank you, Antonida Vasilyevna.'

'And you, Potapych, you go and tell that fool of a waiter to find me a suitable suite of rooms. They must be well decorated, and not too high up. Have my luggage taken up to them. But what are they all falling over themselves for? Why are they all creeping about? What grovellers these fellows are! Who's that with you?' she added, turning back to me.

'A Mr Astley,' I replied.

'And who is Mr Astley?'

'A traveller like me, and my very good friend, as well as an acquaintance of the General's.'

'Oh, an Englishman? So that's why he was staring at me without opening his mouth. Well, I like Englishmen. Now, take me upstairs, straight to their rooms. Where are they lodging?'

Madame was lifted up in her chair by the flunkeys, and I preceded her up the grand staircase. Our progress attracted a lot of attention, and everyone we met stopped to stare at the procession. It happened that the hotel had the reputation of being the best, the most expensive and the most aristocratic in the whole spa, and at every turn on the staircase or in the corridors we encountered fine ladies and important-looking Englishmen – more than one of whom hurried downstairs to inquire of the awestruck head waiter who the newcomer was. To all such questions he gave the same answer – namely, that the old lady was an influential foreigner, a Russian, a countess, and a *grande dame*, and that she had taken the suite which, during the previous week, had been occupied by the Grand Duchess de N.

Meanwhile Grandmother, the cause of all the sensation, was being borne aloft in her armchair. Every person she met she scanned with an inquisitive eye, after first of all interrogating me about him or her at the top of her voice. She was quite stout, and, though she could not leave her chair, one felt, the moment that one first looked at her, that she was also quite tall. Her back was as straight as a board, and she never leant back in her seat. Also, her large grey head, with its sharp, rugged features, she kept always erect as she looked about her in an imperious, challenging sort of way, with expressions and gestures that were completely unaffected. Though she had reached her seventy-sixth year, her face was still fresh, and her teeth had not decayed. She was dressed in a black silk gown and white mobcap.

'I find her tremendously interesting,' whispered Mr Astley as he walked along beside me. Meanwhile I was reflecting that probably the old lady knew all about the telegrams, and even about De Griers, though little or nothing about Mademoiselle Blanche. I said as much to Mr Astley.

But what a wicked man I am! No sooner had I got over my surprise than I found myself rejoicing in the shock we were about to give the

General. I enjoyed the thought so much that I marched ahead as happy as could be.

Our party had lodgings on the second floor. Without knocking, or in any way announcing our presence, I threw open the doors and Grandmother was borne through them in triumph. As if by design, the whole party chanced at that moment to be assembled in the General's study. It was twelve o'clock, and it seemed that an outing of some sort, in which some of the party were to drive in carriages and others to ride on horseback, accompanied by one or two extraneous acquaint-ances, was being planned. The General was there, and also Polina, the children, their nanny, De Griers, Mademoiselle Blanche (in riding-habit), her mother, a young Prince, and some learned German traveller I was meeting for the first time. Into the midst of this assembly the flunkeys carted Madame in her chair, and set her down about three steps away from the General.

My goodness, I'll never forget the spectacle that followed! Just before our entry, the General had been holding forth to the company, and De Griers had been correcting him. I may also mention that, for the last two or three days, Mademoiselle Blanche and De Griers had been making a great deal of the young Prince, under the very nose of the poor General. In short, the mood of the company, though formal and conventional, was happy and conversational. But no sooner did Grandmother appear than the General stopped dead in the middle of what he was saying, and, mouth agape, just stared at the old lady, his eyes almost popping out of his head and his expression frozen as if he had just looked a basilisk[18] in the eyes. In return, Grandmother stared at him silently and without moving, though with a look combining challenge, triumph and ridicule in her eyes. For ten seconds the pair of them remained like that, just looking at one another amidst the profound silence of the company; even De Griers sat there frozen, an extraordinary look of uneasiness creeping over his face. As for Mademoiselle Blanche, she too stared wildly at Grandmother, with her eyebrows raised and her lips parted, while the Prince and the German savant contemplated the tableau in complete bewilderment. Polina looked utterly surprised and bewildered, but in a moment she too turned as white as a sheet, and then her cheeks flushed. Truly, Grandmother's arrival seemed to be a catastrophe for everybody! For my own part, I stood looking from Grandmother to the company and back again, while Mr Astley, as usual, remained in the background, and gazed calmly and politely at what was going on.

'Well, here I am, instead of a telegram!' exclaimed Grandmother at last, to break the silence. 'What? You weren't expecting me?'

'Antonida Vasilyevna! Auntie! But how on earth did you . . . did you . . .?' The unhappy General's mutterings faded away to silence. I really believe that if Grandmother had held her tongue a few seconds longer he would have had a stroke.

'How on earth did I do *what*? Why, I just got on to the train and came here. What else is the railway meant for? But you were all thinking I'd turned up my toes and left my property to you. Oh, I know all about the telegrams you've been sending. They must have cost you a pretty penny, I should think; it isn't cheap to send telegrams from abroad. Well, I just got up and came here. Who's this Frenchman? Monsieur de Griers, I suppose?'

'Oui, madame,' said De Griers. 'Et, croyez, je suis si enchanté! Votre santé . . ., c'est un miracle . . . vous voir ici. Une surprise charmante!'[19]

'Oh, yes, it's "charming", I'm sure! I happen to know you're a complete charlatan. I wouldn't trust you as much as *this*.' She indicated her little finger. 'And who's *she*?' she went on, turning towards Mademoiselle Blanche. Evidently the Frenchwoman looked so becoming in her riding-habit, with her whip in her hand, that she'd made an impression on the old lady. 'Who's that woman there?'

'Mademoiselle de Cominges,' I said. 'And this is her mother, Madame de Cominges. They too are staying in the hotel.'

'Is the daughter married?' asked the old lady, without the least ceremony.

'No,' I replied as respectfully as possible, but in a low voice.

'Is she good company?'

I didn't understand the question.

'I mean, is she or isn't she a bore? Can she speak Russian? When this De Griers was in Moscow, he soon learnt to make himself understood.'

I explained to the old lady that Mademoiselle Blanche had never visited Russia.

'Bonjour, then,' said Grandmother, suddenly turning towards Mademoiselle Blanche.

'Bonjour, madame,' replied Mademoiselle Blanche with an elegant, ceremonious bow while, under cover of an unusual degree of modesty, she endeavoured to express, both by her face and her body, her extreme surprise at such strange behaviour on the part of Grandmother.

'Oh, look how she's casting her eyes down! Look how she's putting on airs and graces! What a give-away! An actress of some sort, to be sure,' was Grandmother's comment. Then she turned suddenly to the General, and continued: 'I've taken up residence here, so I'm going to be your neighbour. Are you glad to hear that, or aren't you?'

'My dear Aunt, believe me when I say that I am, sincerely, deeply, delighted,' replied the General, who had now, to a certain extent, recovered his senses, and given that he could, when the need arose, speak with fluency and gravity and with a certain effect, he set himself to be expansive in his remarks, and went on: 'We have been so dismayed and upset by the news of your indisposition! We had received such hopeless telegrams about you! Then suddenly—'

'Lies, all lies!' interrupted Grandmother.

'But why on earth did you decide to make the journey?' continued the General, raising his voice as he tried to overlook the old lady's last remark. 'Surely, at your age, and in your present state of health, the thing is so unexpected that our surprise is at least understandable. However, I'm glad to see you, as indeed, we all are' – this he said with a dignified, yet conciliatory, smile – 'and will try my best to make your stay here as pleasant as possible.'

'Enough of that! All that is just empty words. You're talking nonsense as usual. I'll know quite well how to pass my time. How did I come to undertake the journey, you ask? Well, is there anything so very surprising about it? It was done quite simply. What is everyone going into raptures about? How are you, Praskovya? What are *you* doing here?'

'And how are *you*, Grandmother?' replied Polina, walking over to the old lady. 'Was the journey long?'

'That's the most sensible question I've been asked yet! Everyone else has just gone "Oooh!" and "Aah!". Well, I'll tell you how it all came about. I lay in bed and lay in bed, and was treated by this doctor and that doctor, until at last I chased the doctors away and called in an apothecary from St Nicholas who had cured an old woman of an illness similar to my own, cured her merely with some hayseed. Well, he did me a great deal of good, and on the third day I sweated the whole malady away and was able to get out of bed. Then my German doctors held another consultation, put on their spectacles and told me that if I would go abroad and take a course of the waters, the indisposition would eventually disappear completely. "Why should it not?" I thought to myself. So I got everything arranged, and on the following day, a Friday, set out for here, with Potapych and a maid. I brought Fyodor the footman as well, but I sent him back from Berlin as I realised I didn't need him. I had a private compartment in the train, and whenever I had to change I always found porters at the station who were ready to carry me for a few coppers. You have nice rooms here,' she went on, looking round. 'But where on earth did you get the money for them, my good sir? I thought everything of yours had been mortgaged. This Frenchman alone must be your creditor for a good deal. Oh, I know all about it, all about it.'

'I – I'm surprised at you, Auntie,' said the General in some confusion. 'I – I'm really surprised. But I don't need any help to look after my finances. In any case, my expenses do not exceed my income, and we—'

'They don't exceed it? What? Why, you're robbing your children of their last kopeck – you, their guardian!'

'After that,' said the General, completely taken aback, 'after what you've just said, I don't know whether—'

'You're right, you don't. Good heavens, are you never going to give up that roulette-playing of yours? Are you going to squander all your property?'

This made such an impression on the General that he almost choked with fury.

'Roulette, indeed? Me, play roulette? Really, in view of my position . . . Just think what you're saying, Auntie. You must still be ill.'

'Rubbish, rubbish!' she retorted. 'The truth is that you *cannot* be dragged away from that roulette. You're lying. This very day I mean to go and see for myself what roulette is like. Praskovya, tell me what there is to be seen around here; and you, Alexei Ivanovich, you show me the sights; and you, Potapych, make a list of excursions for me. What *is* there to see here?' she inquired of Polina again.

'There's a ruined castle, and the Schlangenberg.'

'The Schlangenberg? What's that? A forest?'

'No, a mountain. At the peak, there's a place they've fenced off. There's a really beautiful view from there.'

'Could a chair be carried up this mountain of yours?'

'No doubt we could find porters for the purpose,' I butted in.

At this moment Fedosya, the nursemaid, approached the old lady with the General's children.

'No, I don't want to see them,' said Grandmother. 'I hate kissing children, they've always got runny noses. How are you getting on, Fedosya?'

'I am very well, thank you, Madame,' replied the nursemaid. 'And how is your ladyship? We have been feeling so anxious about you!'

'Yes, I know, you good soul. But who are those other guests?' the old lady continued, turning again to Polina. 'For instance, who is that old rascal in the glasses?'

'Prince Nilsky, Grandmother,' whispered Polina.

'Oh, a Russian? I'd no idea he'd be able to understand me! I hope he didn't hear what I said. As for Mr Astley, I've seen him already, and I see he's here again. How do you do?' she added to the gentleman in question.

Mr Astley bowed in silence.

'Have you *nothing* to say to me?' the old lady went on. 'Say something, for goodness sake! Translate for him, Polina.'

Polina did so.

'I have only to say,' replied Mr Astley gravely, but with alacrity, 'that I am indeed glad to see you in such good health.' This was interpreted to Grandmother, and she seemed very pleased.

'How well English people know how to answer one!' she remarked. 'That's why I like them so much better than those Frenchies. Come and see me,' she added to Mr Astley. 'I'll try not to bore you too much. Polina, translate that for me and tell him I'm staying in rooms on a lower floor. Yes, on – a – lower – floor,' she repeated to Astley, pointing downwards with her finger.

Astley looked pleased at receiving the invitation.

Next, the old lady looked Polina up and down, from head to foot, with careful attention.

'I could come to like you, Praskovya,' she suddenly remarked, 'you're a nice girl, the best of the lot. You have some character about you. I, too, have character. Turn round. That's not false hair you're wearing, is it?'

'No, Grandmother. It's my own.'

'That's good. I don't like the stupid fashions of today. You're very pretty. I would have fallen in love with you if I'd been a man. Why aren't you married? Well, it's time I was going now. I want to walk, but I always have to ride. Are you still in a bad mood?' she added to the General.

'Not at all,' replied the now mollified General.

'I quite understand that at your time of life . . .'

'Cette vieille est tombée en enfance,'[20] De Griers whispered to me.

'I want to look round a little,' the old lady added to the General. 'Will you lend me Alexei Ivanovich for the purpose?'

'As much as you like. But I myself – yes, and Polina and Monsieur de Griers, too – we all of us hope to have the pleasure of escorting you.'

'Mais, madame, cela sera un plaisir,'[21] De Griers commented with a bewitching smile.

'A "pleasure" indeed! You amuse me, monsieur.' Then she said to the General: 'You're not getting any of my money, you know. Well, I must be off to my rooms now, to see what they're like. Afterwards we'll have a little look round. Come on, lift me up.'

Again Grandmother was lifted up and carried down the staircase in the midst of a crowd of followers. The General was walking as if he had been hit on the head with a club, and De Griers seemed to be plunged deep in thought. Mademoiselle Blanche was going to stay behind but thought better of it and followed the rest, with the Prince in her wake. Only the German and Madame de Cominges remained in the General's apartments.

X

At spas – all over Europe, it seems – hotel owners and head waiters are guided in their allotment of rooms to visitors, not so much by the wishes and requirements of the visitors as by the hoteliers' opinion of the guests. It may also be said that they seldom make a mistake. Grandmother, however, was for some reason or another allotted such a sumptuous suite that it really went too far, her suite consisting of four magnificently appointed rooms, with a bathroom, servants' quarters, a separate room for her maid, and so on. In fact, during the previous week the suite had been occupied by no less a personage than a Grand Duchess, which circumstance was duly explained to the new occupant as an excuse for raising the price of these apartments. Grandmother had herself carried – or, rather, wheeled – through each room in turn, so that she might subject the whole suite to a close and careful scrutiny, while the head waiter (an elderly, bald-headed man) walked respectfully by her side.

What everyone took Grandmother to be I do not know, but it appeared, at least, that she was deemed to be a person not only of great importance, but also, and even more so, of great wealth; and without delay they entered her in the hotel register as 'Madame la Générale, Princesse de Tarassevitcheva', though she'd never been a princess in her life. Her retinue, her reserved compartment in the train, her pile of quite unnecessary trunks, suitcases and chests, all helped to increase her prestige; while her wheeled chair, her sharp tone of voice, her eccentric questions (asked with an air of the most overbearing and unbridled imperiousness), her whole bearing – outspoken, abrupt and imperious as it was – put the finishing touches to the general awe in which she was held. As she inspected her new abode, she ordered her chair to be stopped from time to time so that, with her finger extended towards some article of furniture, she might ply the head waiter, who kept smiling respectfully but was clearly becoming quite unnerved, with unexpected questions. She addressed them to him in

French, although her pronunciation of the language was so bad that sometimes I had to translate them for her. For the most part, the head waiter's answers were unsatisfactory and failed to please her; not that the questions themselves were of any importance, generally relating to God knows all what. For instance, on one occasion she stopped in front of a picture, a poor copy of a well-known original with a mythological subject.

'Who is this a portrait of?' she inquired.

The head waiter explained that it was probably some countess or other.

'But why don't you know who?' the old lady retorted. 'You live here, but you can't say for certain who it is! And why is the picture there at all? And why are her eyes squinting like that?'

To all these questions the head waiter could give no satisfactory reply, despite his flustered attempts to do so.

'What a fool!' exclaimed Grandmother in Russian. Then she proceeded on her way, only to repeat the same performance in front of a Dresden figurine which she looked at for a long time and then, for some reason or another, ordered them to take away. Finally, she inquired of the head waiter what the rugs in her bedroom were worth and where they had been manufactured; the head waiter could do no more than promise to make inquiries.

'What donkeys these people are!' she commented. Next, she turned her attention to the bed.

'What a huge counterpane!' she exclaimed. 'Turn it back, please.' The servants did so.

'A bit further. Even further yet. Turn it *right* back. And take off those pillows and bolsters, and lift up the feather bed.'

The bed was unmade for her inspection.

'Thank goodness there are no bugs,' she remarked.

'Take all the bedding off, and then put on my own pillows and sheets. But really, this place is too luxurious for an old woman like me. It's too large for just one person. Alexei Ivanovich, come and see me whenever you aren't teaching your pupils.'

'Since yesterday, I am no longer in the General's service,' I replied, 'but merely living in the hotel on my own account.'

'Why is that?'

'Because, the other day, there arrived here from Berlin a German Baron and his wife the Baroness, people of some importance; and, it chanced that, when taking a walk, I spoke to them in German without keeping to a Berlin accent.'

'Well, what of it?'

'This action on my part the Baron considered an insult, and complained about it to the General, who yesterday dismissed me from his employ.'

'But did you swear at this precious Baron, or something like that? Not that it would matter even if you did.'

'No, I didn't. On the contrary, it was the Baron who raised his stick at me.'

At that, Grandmother turned sharply to the General.

'What? And you, you crawler, you allowed your tutor to be treated like that? And then dismissed him from his post? You're soft in the head, the whole lot of you! I can see that for myself.'

'Don't you worry, Auntie,' the General replied with a tone of condescending familiarity. 'I'm quite capable of managing my own affairs. Moreover, Alexei Ivanovich hasn't given you an entirely accurate account of the matter.'

'What did you do next?' the old lady inquired of me.

'I was going to challenge the Baron to a duel,' I replied as modestly as possible, 'but the General objected to my doing so.'

'And *why* did you object?' she asked the General. Then she turned to the head waiter and said, 'You might as well go. Come back when I call for you. There's no point in you just standing there gawping. I can't stand that awful German face of yours.' At this, the head waiter bowed and left, clearly not having understood Grandmother's compliments.

'Pardon me, Auntie,' the General continued, with a smirk on his face, 'but surely duels aren't allowed.'

'Why not? All men are just farmyard cockerels, so they might as well fight. But as I can see, you're all simpletons who can't even stand up for your own country. Come on, lift me up. Potapych, see to it that you always have *two* porters ready and waiting. Go and hire them now. There's no need for more than two, because I will only need to be carried upstairs. On the level or in the street I can be wheeled along. Go and tell them that, and pay them in advance, so that they'll show me some respect. And Potapych, you are always to accompany me, and *you*, Alexei Ivanovich, are to point out the Baron to me while we are out. I'd like to get a squint at this precious 'von Baron' fellow. And where does one go to play roulette?'

I explained to her that the game was played in the salons of the casino, whereupon there followed a string of questions about whether there were many such salons, whether many people played in them, whether those people played for a whole day at a time, and whether the game was played according to fixed rules. At length, I thought it best to say that the most advisable course would be for her to go and see for herself, since a mere description of it would be a difficult matter.

'Then take me straight there,' she said. 'You lead the way, Alexei Ivanovich.'

'What, Auntie? Before you've even rested from your journey?' the General inquired solicitously. For some reason that I couldn't fathom, he seemed to be getting nervous; indeed, the whole party was showing signs of anxiety and exchanging glances with one another. Probably they were thinking that it would be an awkward, even embarrassing, business to accompany Grandmother to the casino, where, very likely, she would come out with more of her eccentricities, and in public too! But on their own initiative they'd offered to escort her!

'Why should I take a rest?' she retorted. 'I'm not tired, I've been sitting still these past five days. Let's see what the medicinal springs and spa waters are like, and where to find them. And what about that . . . that . . . what did you call it, Praskovya? – you know, that place at the top of the mountain? The peak, was it?'

'Yes, the peak, Grandmother.'

'Yes, the peak, then. Is there anything else for me to see here?'

'Oh, yes, certainly, a lot of things,' replied Polina, slightly embarrassed.

'But you don't know what they are, is that it? Marfa, *you* must come with me as well,' went on the old lady to her maid.

'No, no, Auntie!' exclaimed the General. 'Really, she cannot come. They wouldn't even admit Potapych to the casino.'

'Rubbish! Just because she's my servant, is that a reason for leaving her out? She's a human being just like the rest of us, and as she's been travelling with me for the past week she might like to look around. Who else could she go out with but me? She would never dare to show her nose in the street alone.'

'But, Auntie . . .'

'Are you ashamed to be seen with me? You stay at home, then, and you'll be asked no questions. A fine General *you* are, to be sure! I'm a general's widow myself. But, then, why should I drag the whole party with me? I'll go and see the sights with just Alexei Ivanovich to escort me.'

De Griers strongly insisted that *everyone* ought to accompany her. Indeed, he launched into a perfect shower of charming phrases concerning the pleasure of accompanying her, and so forth. Everyone was touched by his words.

'Mais elle est tombée en enfance,' he added quietly to the General. 'Seule, elle fera des bêtises . . .'[22] I couldn't hear any more than that, but he seemed to have got some plan in mind, and even to be feeling his hopes returning.

It was about half a mile to the casino, and our route led us through the chestnut-tree avenue to the square directly in front of the building. The General, I could see, was somewhat reassured by the fact that, though our progress was quite eccentric in its nature, it was, at least, proper and orderly. As a matter of fact, the spectacle of a person who is unable to walk is nothing to cause surprise at a spa. Yet it was clear that the General had a great fear of the casino itself: for why should a person who had lost the use of her limbs, more especially an old woman, be going to rooms which were set apart only for roulette? On either side of the wheeled chair walked Polina and Mademoiselle Blanche, the latter smiling modestly and making jokes, and, in short, making herself so agreeable to Grandmother that in the end the old lady relented towards her. On the other side of the chair, Polina had to answer an endless flow of trivial questions, such as 'Who was that who passed just now?', 'Who's that coming along?', 'Is this a large town?', 'Are the public gardens large?', 'What sort of trees are those?', 'What's the name of those hills?', 'Are those eagles I can see flying over yonder?', 'What's that stupid-looking building?', and so on. Meanwhile Astley whispered to me, as he walked by my side, that he was expecting a lot to happen that morning. Behind the old lady's chair marched Potapych and Marfa – Potapych in his frockcoat and white waistcoat, but wearing a cap, and the forty-year-old, rosy-cheeked, but slightly greying, Marfa in a mobcap, cotton dress and squeaky shoes. Frequently the old lady would twist round to speak to these servants. As for De Griers, he was speaking as though he had made up his mind to do something (though it's also possible that he was speaking that way merely to reassure the General, with whom he appeared to be discussing something). But, alas, Grandmother had uttered the fatal words, 'I am not going to give you any of my money', and though De Griers might regard these words lightly, the General knew his aunt better. I also noticed that De Griers and Mademoiselle Blanche were still exchanging looks, while I lost sight of the Prince and the German savant at the far end of the avenue, where they had turned back and left us.

Into the casino we marched in triumph. Immediately, both the doorman and the footmen showed us the same respect as the flunkeys in the hotel had done. Yet it was not without some curiosity that they looked at us. Without wasting time, Grandmother gave orders that she should be wheeled through every room in the establishment, praising a few, indifferent to most, but asking questions about everything. Finally we reached the gaming-rooms, where a footman who was standing guard at the doors flung them open with a flourish.

Grandmother's entry into the roulette room made a profound impression on the public. Around the tables, and at the far end of the room where the trente-et-quarante table was set out, there may have been a hundred and fifty to two hundred gamblers, standing several rows deep. Those who had managed to push their way to the tables were standing with their feet firmly planted, so to avoid having to give up their places until they had finished their game (since merely to stand watching, and so occupy a gambler's place to no purpose, was not permitted). True, chairs were provided around the tables, but few players made use of them, more especially if there was a large number of the general public present, since standing allowed one to get closer, and therefore to have a better opportunity to make calculations and place bets. Behind the front row were crowded a second and third row of people waiting their turn, but sometimes their impatience led these people to stretch a hand through the first row in order to place their stakes. Even people in the third row back would push themselves forward to place a bet, for which reason hardly more than five or ten minutes passed without some scene arising over disputed money at one end of the table or other. The casino police are an able body of men, though. It's impossible to avoid this crowding – not that the owners want to, as it's very profitable – but the eight croupiers appointed to each table keep an eye on the bets, make the necessary calculations and generally settle disputes as they arise. As a last resort they call in the casino police, and the matter is sorted out immediately. Policemen are stationed around the casino in plain clothes and mingle with the spectators, so it's impossible to spot them. In particular they keep a look-out for pickpockets and swindlers, who simply swan into the salons and reap a rich harvest. In fact, money is being pinched all the time, though, of course, if the attempt goes wrong, there's a terrible uproar. Generally, one need only go up to a roulette table, begin to play, and then openly grab someone else's winnings; if a row starts, the thief insists loudly that the stake was *his*; and if the attempt has been carried out with sufficient skill, and the witnesses waver in their testimony, the thief as likely as not succeeds in getting away with the money, provided the sum involved is not a large one – anything larger the croupiers or some fellow-player will have been keeping an eye on. Moreover, if it's a stake of insignificant size, its true owner will sometimes decline to continue the argument rather than become involved in a scandal. On the other hand, if the thief is detected, he is ignominiously thrown out.

All this Grandmother watched with frank curiosity; and, when some thieves happened to be thrown out, she was delighted. Trente-et-quarante didn't interest her much; she preferred roulette with its ever-spinning wheel. At length she expressed a wish to take a closer look at the game; whereupon, in some mysterious manner, the footmen and some other officious people (especially some Poles of the kind who, after losing their money, offer their services to successful gamblers and especially to foreigners) at once cleared a space for the old lady among the crush, at the very centre of one of the tables, next to the chief croupier, after which they wheeled her chair there. At this, a number of visitors who were not playing but only looking on (particu-larly some Englishmen and their families) pressed forward closer to the table in order to watch the old lady from among the ranks of the gamblers. Many a lorgnette I saw turned in her direction and the croupiers' hopes rose high that such an eccentric player was about to provide them with something out of the ordinary. An old lady of seventy-five years who, though unable to walk, wanted to play, was not something you saw every day. I, too, pressed forward towards the table, and placed myself by Grandmother's side; while Marfa and Potapych remained somewhere in the background among the crowd, and the General, Polina and De Griers, with Mademoiselle Blanche, also remained hidden among the spectators.

At first the old lady did no more than watch the gamblers, and ply me, in a half-whisper, with questions: 'Who's he? Who's she?' She was particularly interested in a very young man who was betting heavily and had won (so the word was going round) as much as forty thousand francs, which were lying in front of him on the table in a heap of gold and banknotes. His eyes were flashing, and his hands were shaking, but all the while he placed bets without any sort of calculation – just what came to his hand, as he kept on winning and winning, just raking it in again and again. Footmen fussed over him, putting a chair just behind where he was standing and clearing the spectators from around him so that he would have more room and not be crowded – all this done, of course, in the hope of a generous tip: gamblers sometimes hand out tips without even looking to see what's in their hand. Beside him stood a Pole in a state of respectful agitation, who, also in expectation of a generous tip, kept whispering to him at intervals (probably telling him what to stake, and advising and directing his play). Yet never once did the player even glance at him as he placed bet after bet and raked in his winnings. Evidently, he was dead to everything else.

For a few minutes Grandmother watched him.

'Go and tell him,' she suddenly exclaimed, nudging me, 'go and tell him to stop now and take his money and go home. He'll start losing soon, losing everything he's won so far.' She seemed almost breathless with excitement. 'Where's Potapych?' she continued. 'Send Potapych to speak to him. No, *you* must tell him, you must tell him,' here she prodded me again, 'because I've no idea where Potapych is. Sortez, sortez[23],' she shouted to the young man, until I leant over to her and whispered in her ear that shouting was not allowed, not even talking loudly, because it disturbed the players' calculations, and might lead to our being thrown out.

'How provoking!' she retorted. 'Then the young man is doomed! I suppose he *wants* to be ruined. Yet I can't bear to see him have to hand it all back. What a fool he is!' and the old lady turned sharply away.

Over to the left, among the players at the other half of the table, there was a young lady playing, with a dwarf beside her. Who the dwarf may have been – whether a relative or someone she just brought with her for effect – I don't know, but I'd noticed her there on previous occasions, since, every day, she entered the casino at precisely one o'clock and left again at two, playing for exactly one hour. Being well known to the attendants, she always had a seat provided for her, and taking some gold and a few thousand-franc notes out of her pocket would begin to bet quietly, calmly, with many calculations and jotting down figures in pencil on a piece of paper, as though trying to work out a system according to which, at given moments, the odds might group themselves. She always staked large sums of money, and either lost or won one, two or three thousand francs a day, but never more than that, after which she would leave. Grandmother took a long look at her.

'*That* woman is not losing,' she said. 'What's her family? Do you know her? Who is she?'

'She is, I believe, a Frenchwoman, of a certain background,' I replied.

'Ah, yes. You can tell a bird by its behaviour. I can see she's got sharp claws. Now, explain to me the meaning of each round in the game, and how one ought to place bets.'

I began to explain the meaning of all the combinations, of 'rouge' and 'noir', of 'pair' and 'impair', of 'manque' and 'passe' with, lastly, the different values in the system of numbers. Grandmother listened attentively, took notes, asked various questions and quickly got the hang of it. Indeed, since example of each system of betting kept coming up, a great deal of information could be assimilated easily and quickly. Grandmother was extremely pleased.

'But what's zero?' she inquired. 'Just now I heard the fair-haired croupier call out "zero". And why has he raked in all the money on the table? How can he take the whole pile for himself! What does zero mean?'

'"Zero" means the bank wins. If the wheel stops at that figure, everything lying on the table goes to the bank.'

'Then I would get nothing if I had placed a bet?'

'No, unless by any chance you had *deliberately* bet on zero, in which case you would get thirty-five times the value of your stake.'

'Why thirty-five times, when zero turns up so often? And if so, why do more of these fools not bet on it?'

'Because the chances against its occurrence is thirty-six to one.'

'Rubbish! Potapych, where's Potapych? Wait a moment, I can give you some money myself.' The old lady took out of her pocket a tightly-clasped purse, and extracted from its depths a gold friedrich[24]. 'Go and put that on zero.'

'But, Grandmother, zero has only this very moment turned up,' I remonstrated, 'so it may not do so again for ever so long. Wait a little while, and then you may have a better chance.'

'Rubbish! Place the bet, please.'

'Excuse me, but zero might not turn up again until, say, tonight, even though you had staked thousands on it. It often happens like that.'

'Rubbish, rubbish! He who fears the wolf should never enter the forest. What? Have we lost? Then bet again.'

We lost a second friedrich, and then I put down a third. Grandmother could scarcely stay seated in her chair, so intent was she on the little ball as it leapt through the notches of the ever-spinning wheel. However, the third gold friedrich followed the first two. Grandmother was beside herself, she couldn't sit still and actually thumped the table with her fist when the croupier called out 'Thirty-six' instead of the desired zero.

'Oh, listen to that!' fumed the old lady. 'When will that damn zero turn up again? I won't budge until I see it. I do believe that damned croupier is deliberately stopping it turning up. Alexei Ivanovich, bet two gold friedrichs this time. The moment we stop placing bets, that's when that blasted zero will turn up again, and we'll get nothing.'

'But, Grandmother . . .'

'Place the bet, will you! It's not *your* money.'

Accordingly I staked two gold coins. The ball went hopping round the wheel until it began to settle in the holes. Meanwhile Grandmother sat as though turned to stone, with my hand clutched tightly in hers.

'Zero!' called the croupier.

'There! You see, you see!' cried the old lady, as she turned and faced me, wreathed in smiles. 'I told you so! It was the Lord God himself who suggested to me to wager those two coins. Now, how much should I get? Why aren't they paying me my winnings? Potapych! Marfa! Where are they? What has become of our group? Potapych, Potapych!'

'Later, Grandmother,' I whispered. 'Potapych is outside; they wouldn't let him into these rooms. Look! You're being paid your money. Here you are.' The croupiers tossed over a heavy roll of banknotes wrapped in blue paper, amounting to fifty gold friedrichs, together with another twenty single coins. I passed it all to the old lady in a money-shovel.

'Faites le jeu, messieurs! Faites le jeu, messieurs! Rien ne va plus?'[25] called the croupier as once more he invited the company to bet and prepared to turn the wheel.

'We'll be too late! He's going to spin it again! Place a bet, place a bet!' Grandmother was in an absolute fever. 'Don't hang back! Be quick!' She was almost beside herself, and pushed me as hard as she could.

'What should I bet on, Grandmother?'

'On zero, on zero! On zero again! Stake as much as you can. How much have we got? Seventy gold friedrichs? We won't miss them, so stake twenty at a time.'

'But think for a moment, Grandmother. Sometimes zero doesn't turn up for two hundred rounds in a row. I warn you, you may lose all your money.'

'You're wrong, completely wrong. Place the bet, I tell you! What a jabberer you are! I know perfectly well what I'm doing.' The old lady was shaking with excitement.

'But the rules don't allow more than twelve friedrichs to be bet on zero at any one time.'

'What do you mean, "don't allow"? Surely you've got that wrong? Monsieur, monsieur' – here she poked the croupier who was sitting on her left, preparing to spin the wheel – 'Combien zéro? Douze? Douze?'[26]

I translated for her.

'Yes, Madame,' was the croupier's polite reply. 'In the same way that no single stake can exceed four thousand florins. That's the rules.'

'Then there's nothing else for it. Bet twelve friedrichs.'

'Le jeu est fait!'[27] the croupier called out. The wheel spun, and stopped at thirty. We'd lost!

'Again, again, again! Place the bet again!' shouted the old lady.

Without attempting to oppose her further, but merely shrugging my shoulders, I placed twelve more friedrichs on the table. The wheel whirled round and round, with Grandmother simply shaking as she watched it spinning.

'Does she think that zero is going to be the winning number again?' I thought as I stared at her in astonishment. Yet there was a look of absolute certainty of winning on her face; she looked perfectly convinced that zero was about to come up again. At length the ball dropped off into one of the holes.

'Zero!' cried the croupier.

'Yes!!!' screamed the old lady, as she turned to me in triumph.

I myself was at heart a gambler. At that moment I became acutely conscious both of that fact and of the fact that my hands and knees were shaking and the blood was hammering in my brain. Of course, this was a rare occasion, an occasion on which zero had turned up no less than three times within a dozen rounds; yet there was nothing so very surprising in such an occurrence, seeing that, only three days ago, I myself had seen zero turning up *three times in succession*, and one of the players who was recording the winning numbers on paper had commented that for several days before that zero had never turned up at all!

With Grandmother, as with anyone who has won a very large sum of money, the management settled up with great care and attention. She was due no less than four hundred and twenty friedrichs, that is to say four thousand florins and twenty friedrichs. The twenty friedrichs were paid to her in gold, and the florins in banknotes.

This time the old lady did not call for Potapych, because she was too preoccupied with what was going on. Not outwardly shaken by what had occurred, she seemed perfectly calm (she was, one might say, trembling on the inside). At length, totally intent on the game, she burst out:

'Alexei Ivanovich, did the croupier not just say that four thousand florins were the most that could be staked at any one time? Well, take the four thousand and stake them on red.'

It was useless to argue with her. Once more the wheel spun.

'Rouge!' called out the croupier.

That was another four thousand florins, making eight thousand in all!

'Give me four thousand,' commanded Grandmother, 'and stake the other four thousand on red again.'

I did so.

'Rouge!' announced the croupier again.

'Twelve thousand!' cried the old lady. 'Give me the whole lot. Put the gold into this purse here, and hide the banknotes. Well, that's enough! Let's go home. Wheel my chair away.'

XI

The chair, with the old lady in it, beaming widely, was wheeled away towards the doors at the far end of the salon, while our party hastened to crowd round her and offer her their congratulations. In fact, eccentric as her behaviour was, it was entirely made up for by her triumph, with the result that the General no longer feared to be publicly compromised by being seen with such a strange woman but, smiling in a condescending, cheerfully familiar way, as though he were soothing a child, he offered his congratulations to the old lady. At the same time, both he and the rest of the spectators were clearly impressed. All around us, people were pointing to Grandmother and talking about her. Many people even walked past her chair, in order to get a closer look at her while, at a little distance, Astley was carrying on a conversation on the subject with two English acquaintances of his. A number of fine ladies were staring at Grandmother as if she were some sort of curiosity. De Griers showered her with smiles and congratulations.

'Quelle victoire!'[28] exclaimed De Griers.

'Mais, Madame, c'était du feu!'[29] added Mademoiselle Blanche with an ingratiating smile.

'Yes, indeed, I've just won twelve thousand florins,' replied the old lady. 'Not forgetting this gold. With that, it ought to come to nearly thirteen thousand. How much is that in Russian money? Six thousand roubles, is that about it?'

I calculated that the sum would amount to more than seven thousand roubles, or, at the present rate of exchange, possibly even eight thousand.

'Eight thousand roubles! That's splendid! And to think of you simpletons sitting there and doing nothing! Potapych! Marfa! Look what I've won!'

'How *did* you do it, Madame?' Marfa exclaimed ecstatically. 'Eight thousand roubles!'

'And I'm going to give you fifty gulden each. There you are.'

Potapych and Marfa rushed to kiss her hand.

'And I'll give ten gulden to each of the porters as well. Give them a coin each, Alexei Ivanovich. But why is that footman bowing to me, and that other man as well? Are they congratulating me? Well, let them have a ten-gulden piece each too.'

'Madame la princesse – Un pauvre expatrie – Malheur continuel – Les princes russes sont si genereux!'[30] said a man with a moustache who for some time now had been hanging around the old lady's chair, dressed in a shabby frockcoat and coloured waistcoat, constantly taking off his cap and smiling pathetically.

'Give him ten gulden,' said Grandmother. 'No, give him twenty. Now, enough of this or I'll never be done with it. Lift me up and carry me out. Praskovya, I mean to buy a new dress for you tomorrow. Yes, and for you too, Mademoiselle Blanche. Please translate that for me, Praskovya.'

'Merci, Madame,' replied Mademoiselle Blanche curtsying gratefully as she smiled ironically to De Griers and the General. The latter looked embarrassed, and was greatly relieved when we reached the avenue.

'How surprised Fedosia will be, too!' went on Grandmother (thinking of the General's nanny). 'She, like you, will have the price of a new dress. Here, Alexei Ivanovich! Give that beggar something.' (A hump-backed man in rags had come over to stare at us.)

'But perhaps he's *not* a beggar, just a rogue,' I replied.

'Never mind, never mind. Give him a gulden anyway.'

I went over to the beggar in question and handed him the coin. Looking at me in great astonishment, he took the gulden without a word. He smelt strongly of drink.

'Have you never tried your luck, Alexei Ivanovich?'

'No, Grandmother.'

'But I could see that you were itching to do so, weren't you?'

'I do mean to try my luck soon.'

'Then stake everything on zero. You've seen how it ought to be done. How much money do you have?'

'Two hundred gulden, Grandmother.'

'Not very much. See here, I'll lend you five hundred if you like. Take this purse of mine.' With that she added sharply to the General: 'But *you* needn't expect to get anything.'

This seemed to upset him, but he said nothing, and De Griers just scowled.

'Que diable!' he whispered to the General. 'C'est une terrible vieille.'[31]

'Look! Another beggar, another beggar!' exclaimed Grandmother. 'Alexei Ivanovich, go and give him a gulden too.'

As she spoke, I saw coming towards us a grey-headed old man with a wooden leg, dressed in a blue frockcoat and carrying a staff. He looked like an old soldier. As soon as I offered him the coin, he fell back a step or two and eyed me threateningly.

'Was ist's der Teufel!'[32] he cried, to which he added a dozen more oaths.

'The man's a fool!' exclaimed Grandmother, waving her hand. 'Move on now, I'm simply famished. When we've had lunch, we'll go back again.'

'What?' cried I. 'You're going to play again?'

'What else do you suppose I'm going to do?' she retorted. 'Sit here and watch all of you sulking?'

'Madame,' said De Griers confidentially, 'les chances peuvent tourner. Une seule mauvaise chance, et vous perdrez tout – surtout avec votre jeu. C'était terrible!'[33]

'Vous perdrez absolument,'[34] put in Mademoiselle Blanche.

'What has that got to do with *you*?' retorted the old lady. 'It's not *your* money I'm going to lose, it's my own. And where's that Mr Astley of yours?' she added to me.

'He stayed behind in the casino.'

'What a pity! He's such a nice man!'

Arriving back at the hotel and meeting the head waiter on the staircase, Grandmother called him over and boasted to him of her winnings, thereafter doing the same with Fedosia and giving her thirty gulden, after which she told her to serve lunch. Fedosia and Marfa sang her praises all through lunch.

'I was watching you all the time, Madame,' quavered Marfa, 'and I asked Potapych what Mistress was trying to do. And, my word! the heaps and heaps of money that were lying on the table! I've never seen so much money in my life. And there were gentlefolk round it, and other gentlefolk sitting down. So I asked Potapych where all these gentry had come from, for I thought to myself, maybe the Holy Mother of God will help our mistress in particular among them. Yes, I prayed for you, Madame, and my heart was thumping and I was trembling and trembling. The Lord be with her, I thought to myself; and in answer to my prayer look what He has done for you! Even now I tremble, yes, tremble, to think of it all.'

'Alexei Ivanovich,' said the old lady, 'after dinner, that is to say, about four o'clock, get ready to go out with me again. But for the time being, goodbye. Don't forget to call a doctor, because I must take the waters. On you go and do that or we'll forget all about it.'

When I left Grandmother, I was completely bewildered. I tried in vain to imagine what would become of our party, or what would happen next. I could see that none of the party had yet recovered their presence of mind, least of all the General. Grandmother's appearance instead of the hourly expected telegram announcing her death (with, of course, the resultant legacies) had so disrupted the whole web of plans and projects that it was with decided feelings of apprehension and a growing helplessness that the conspirators viewed the old lady's future performances at the roulette tables. And this second factor was possibly more important than the first, since, though Grandmother had twice declared that she did not intend to give the General any money, that declaration was not grounds for completely abandoning hope. Certainly De Griers, who was up to his neck in the affair with the General, had not totally lost heart, and I felt sure that Mademoiselle Blanche also (Mademoiselle Blanche who was not only as deeply involved as the other two, but was also expecting to become Madame General and so an important legatee) would not give up easily, but would use every resource of her coquetry on the old lady, unlike Polina, who was proud and difficult to understand and lacked the art of ingratiating herself. But now, when Grandmother had just performed an astonishing feat at roulette; now, when the old lady's personality had so clearly and typically revealed itself to be that of a determined, imperious old woman who had 'tombée en enfance'; now, when everything appeared to be lost – why, now Grandmother was as happy as a child and would go on playing until she had lost everything. 'Good Lord!' I thought with, may God forgive me, a malicious smile, 'every gold friedrich Grandmother staked must have blistered the General's heart and maddened De Griers and driven Mademoiselle de Cominges almost crazy at the sight of the cup being dashed from her lips.' Another thing to consider was that when, delighted at winning, Grandmother was distributing alms right, left and centre, taking everyone to be a beggar, she again snapped at the General that he wasn't going to get any of her money, which meant that the old lady had quite made up her mind on the matter, that she was quite certain about it. Yes, there was danger ahead.

All these thoughts passed through my mind during the few moments that, having left the old lady's rooms, I was going up to my own room on the top floor. What most struck me was the fact that, although I had guessed the main, the strongest, threads which united the various actors in the drama, I had, until now, been ignorant of the methods and secrets of the game. For Polina had never been completely open with me. Although, on occasions, it had happened that involuntarily, as it were, she had revealed to me something of her heart, I had noticed that in most cases – in fact, nearly always – she had either laughed away these revelations, or muddled them, or deliberately given them a false slant. Yes, she must have concealed a great deal from me. But I had a feeling that now the end of this strained and mysterious situation was coming. Just one more shock and it would all be over and out in the open. Of my own fortunes, interested though I was in the affair, I took no account at all. I was in the strange position of having no more than two hundred gulden in my possession, of being at a loose end, of having no job, no means of subsistence, not a shred of hope nor any plans for the future, but actually caring nothing about any of these things. Had my mind not been so full of thoughts of Polina, I would have given myself up to the comic interest of the impending outcome, and laughed out loud at it. But the thought of Polina was torture to me. That her fate was settled I already had an inkling, but that was not the thought which was giving me so much distress. What I really wanted was to penetrate her secrets. I wanted her to come to me and say 'I love you', and if she would not come, or if to hope that she would ever do so was an unthinkable absurdity – well, what else is there for me to wish for? Do I really know what I want? I feel like a man who's lost his way. All I want is to be in her presence, and within the circle of her light and splendour – to be there now, and forever, and for the whole of my life. More than that I do not know. How could I ever bring myself to leave her?

On reaching the second floor of the hotel I had a shock. I was just passing the General's suite when something made me look round. There was Polina, coming out of a door about twenty paces away! She hesitated for a moment on seeing me, and then beckoned me to her.

'Polina Alexandrovna!'

'Shhh! Not so loud.'

'Something startled me just now,' I whispered, 'and I looked round and saw you. Some electrical force seems to emanate from your body.'

'Take this letter,' she went on with a frown (she had probably not even heard what I said, she was so preoccupied), 'and hand it personally to Mr Astley. Go as quickly as you can. No answer will be required. He himself . . .' She didn't finish her sentence.

'To Mr Astley?' I asked, in some astonishment. But she'd vanished again.

Aha! So the two were carrying on a correspondence! However, I set off to look for Astley, first at his hotel, and then at the casino, where I went the round of the salons in vain. At length, irritated and almost in despair, I was on my way home when I ran across him among a group of English ladies and gentlemen who had been out for a ride. Beckoning to him to stop, I handed him the letter. We had barely time even to look at one another, before he quickly urged his horse on again, I suspect quite deliberately.

Was jealousy, then, gnawing at me? At all events, I felt extremely depressed, even though I had no desire to find out what the correspondence was about. To think that *he* should be her confidant! 'He's her friend, her close friend!' I thought to myself. But was there any love involved? 'Of course not,' reason whispered to me, but reason counts for little on such occasions. I felt the matter must be cleared up; things were becoming unpleasantly complicated.

I had scarcely set foot in the hotel when the doorman and the head waiter (the latter coming out of his room for the purpose) alike informed me that I was being searched for high and low, that there had been no fewer than three separate messages from the General asking where I was. I was in a fairly foul mood. When I got to his study, I found the General himself there, along with De Griers and Mademoiselle Blanche, but not Mademoiselle's mother, who was a person her reputed daughter used only for show, since in all matters of business the daughter fended for herself and it's unlikely the mother knew anything about what was going on.

There was a very heated discussion in progress, and the door of the study was actually locked, something that didn't usually happen. As I approached the door, I could hear raised voices – the tart, venomous accents of De Griers, Mademoiselle Blanche's excited, impudently abusive tongue, and the General's plaintive wail as he apparently tried to justify himself about something. But when I came to the door, everyone stopped shouting, and tried to put a better face on things. De Griers smoothed his hair and twisted his angry face into a smile, that mean, studiedly polite French smile which I so detest, while the downcast, confused General resumed an air of dignity, though only in a mechanical way. On the other hand, Mademoiselle Blanche did not trouble to conceal the anger that was blazing on her face, but fixed me with a look of impatient expectancy. I may say that up till now she had treated me with complete disdain and far from acknowledging my greetings, had always ignored them.

'Alexei Ivanovich,' began the General in a tone of friendly reproach, 'may I say to you that I find it strange, exceedingly strange, that . . . in short, your conduct towards myself and my family . . . in a word, your, er, extremely . . .'

'Eh! Ce n'est pas ça,' interrupted De Griers in tones of impatience and contempt (evidently he was in charge). 'Mon cher monsieur, notre général se trompe. [35] What he means to say is that he warns you, he begs you most earnestly, not to ruin him. I use that word because—'

'But why? Why?' I interjected.

'Because you have taken it on yourself to act as guide to this, to this – how can I put it? – to this old lady, à cette pauvre terrible vieille[36]. But all she'll do is gamble away everything she has, just gamble it all away. You yourself have seen her play. Once she has acquired the taste for gambling, she'll never leave the roulette table, but out of sheer perversity and temper will bet all she has – and lose it. When people like her gamble, they can never be dragged away from the game, and then . . . and then . . .'

'And then,' said the General, 'you will have ruined my whole family. I and my family are her heirs, because she has no closer relatives than us. I tell you frankly that my affairs are in great, very great, disorder. How much so you yourself are partially aware. If she should lose a large sum or, maybe, her whole fortune, what will become of my children' (here the General exchanged a glance with De Griers) 'or of me?' (here he looked at Mademoiselle Blanche, who turned her head away contemptuously). 'Alexei Ivanovich, I beg of you to save us.'

'Tell me, General, how am I to do that? On what footing do I stand here?'

'Refuse to take her around. Just leave her alone.'

'But she would soon find someone else to take my place, wouldn't she?'

'Ce n'est pas ça, ce n'est pas ça,' De Griers interrupted again, 'que diable![37] We don't want you to leave her alone, but rather to advise her, persuade her, draw her away. At any rate, don't let her gamble, find some counter-attraction for her.'

'And how am I to do that? If only you would undertake the task, Monsieur de Griers,' I said as innocently as possible. At once I saw a quick, excited, questioning glance pass from Mademoiselle Blanche to De Griers, while in the face of the latter there flashed a strange look he couldn't repress.

'Well, at the present moment she would refuse to accept my services,' he said with a wave of his hand. 'But if, later . . .'

Here he gave Mademoiselle Blanche another meaningful glance.

'O mon cher monsieur Alexei, soyez si bon.'[38] Saying this, she advanced towards me with a bewitching smile and grasped and pressed my hands. Hang it all, but how that devilish face of hers could change! At the present moment it was full of supplication, and as gentle in its expression as that of a smiling, roguish infant. She rounded off her sentence with a wink, which the others didn't see. She was clearly trying to bring me to my knees. A crude ploy, really pretty crude.

The General literally leapt up. 'Alexei Ivanovich,' he began, 'pardon me for having said what I did just now, for having said more than I meant to. I do beg and beseech you, I kiss the hem of your garment, as our Russian saying has it, because you, and only you, can save us. I and Mademoiselle de Cominges, we beg of you . . . But you understand the situation, don't you? Surely you understand?' and with his eyes he indicated Mademoiselle Blanche. He looked truly pathetic!

At that moment there were three quiet, polite knocks at the door, which, on being opened, revealed a chambermaid, with Potapych behind her. He had come from Grandmother to request that I should attend her in her rooms. 'She's in a bad mood,' added Potapych.

It was only half-past three.

'My mistress was unable to sleep,' explained Potapych, 'so, after tossing and turning for a while, she suddenly got up, called for her chair and sent me to look for you. She is now waiting at the front door.'

'Quelle mégère!'[39] exclaimed De Griers.

True enough, I found Grandmother in the hotel door, greatly put out at being kept waiting. She had been unable to contain herself until four o'clock.

'Lift me up,' she cried to the porters, and once more we set out for the roulette rooms.

XII

Grandmother was in an impatient, irritable frame of mind. Without doubt the roulette had turned her head, because she seemed to be indifferent to everything else, and, in general, seemed completely distracted. For instance, she didn't ask me any questions about things we saw along the way, except that, when a sumptuous barouche passed us and raised a cloud of dust, she raised her hand for a moment and inquired, 'What was that?' Yet even then she seemed not to hear my reply, although at times her absorption was interrupted by sudden movements and outbursts. When I pointed out to her the Baron and Baroness Burmerhelm walking to the casino, she merely looked at them in an absent-minded sort of way and said 'Oh, yes' with complete indifference. Then, turning sharply to Potapych and Marfa, who were walking behind us, she snapped at them:

'Why are *you* two tagging along? We're not going to take you with us every time. Go back home at once.' Then, when the servants had made hasty bows and departed, she added to me: 'You're all the escort I need.'

At the casino Grandmother seemed to be expected, for no time was lost in getting her her former place beside the croupier. It is my opinion that though croupiers seem such ordinary, humdrum officials – men who couldn't care less whether the bank wins or loses – they are, in reality, anything but indifferent to the bank's losing, and are given instructions to attract players and to keep a watch over the bank's interests, and that for such services, these officials are awarded gifts and bonuses. At all events, the croupiers of Roulettenburg seemed to look on Grandmother as their rightful prey.

And then things turned out exactly as the others had been anticipating they would. This is how it happened:

As soon as we got there, Grandmother ordered me to bet on zero, twelve gold friedrichs at a time. Once, twice, three times I did so, but zero never came up.

'Bet again,' said the old lady, prodding me impatiently in the ribs. I did as I was told.

'How many times have we lost?' she asked, actually grinding her teeth in her excitement.

'That was your twelfth bet. We've lost a hundred and forty-four gold friedrichs,' I replied. 'I'm telling you, Grandmother, zero may not turn up again until tonight.'

'Never mind,' she interrupted. 'Keep on betting on zero, and also put a thousand gulden on red. Here's the money.'

Red turned up, but zero missed again, so we only won back a thousand gulden.

'But you see, you see,' whispered the old lady, 'we've got back almost all we've staked. Try zero again. Let's do it ten more times, and then stop.'

By the fifth round, however, Grandmother was weary of that plan.

'To hell with zero!' she exclaimed. 'Stake four thousand gulden on red.'

'But, Grandmother, that's a huge amount to wager!' I remonstrated. 'Suppose the red doesn't come up?' Grandmother almost hit me in her agitation, which was rapidly making her quarrelsome. Consequently, there was nothing for it but to stake the whole four thousand gulden as she had directed.

The wheel spun while Grandmother sat as upright, and with as proud and calm a look, as though she had not the least doubt of winning.

'Zero!' cried the croupier.

At first the old lady failed to understand the situation, but as soon as she saw the croupier raking in her four thousand gulden, together with everything else that happened to be lying on the table, and recognised that the zero which had been so long turning up, and on which we had lost nearly two thousand gulden, had at last made a sudden reappearance, as if deliberately doing so after she had been abusing it, why then the poor old lady started cursing it and throwing herself about and wailing and gesticulating at the company at large. Indeed, some people near us actually burst out laughing.

'To think that that damned zero should have turned up *now!*' she sobbed. 'That damned, damned number! And it's all *your* fault,' she added, rounding on me in a frenzy. 'It was you who persuaded me to stop betting on it.'

'But, Grandmother, I only explained the game to you. How am I responsible for chance?'

'I'll give you "chance"!' she whispered threateningly. 'Just go away, right now!'

'Goodbye, then, Grandmother.' And I turned to leave.

'No, stay,' she said hastily. 'Where are you going? Why are you leaving me? You fool! No, no . . . stay here. I'm the fool. Tell me what I ought to do.'

'I cannot take it upon myself to advise you, because you'll only blame me if I do so. Play as you please. Tell me exactly what you wish staked, and I will place the bet.'

'Very well. Stake another four thousand gulden on red. Take this banknote to do it with. I've still got twenty thousand roubles in cash.'

'But,' I whispered, 'so much money . . .'

'Never mind. I can't rest until I've won back my losses. Place the bet!'

I placed the bet, and we lost.

'Bet again, bet again – eight thousand at one go!'

'I can't, Grandmother. The largest stake allowed is four thousand gulden.'

'Well, then, stake four thousand.'

This time we won, and Grandmother recovered herself a little.

'You see, you see!' she exclaimed as she nudged me. 'Stake another four thousand.'

I did so, and we lost. And again, and yet again, we lost. 'Grandmother,' I said, 'your twelve thousand gulden are gone.'

'I can see they are,' she replied with, as it were, the calmness of despair. 'I can see they are,' she muttered again, as she gazed straight in front of her, like a person lost in thought. 'Ah well, I don't mean to rest until I've staked another four thousand.'

'But you've no money to do that with, Grandmother. In this bag of yours I can only see a few five per cent bonds and some bills of exchange, but no actual cash.'

'And in the purse?'

'Virtually nothing.'

'But there's a money-changer's office here, isn't there? They told me I would be able to get any sort of paper securities changed here!'

'Certainly you can; any amount you please. But what you'll lose on the transaction would horrify even a Jew!'

'Stuff and nonsense! I'm determined to make good my losses. Take me out of here, and call those fools of bearers.'

I wheeled the chair out of the crowd, and the bearers having duly appeared, we left the casino.

'Hurry, hurry!' commanded Grandmother. 'Show me the nearest way to the money-changer's. Is it far?'

'A few steps, Grandmother.'

At the turning from the square into the avenue we came face to face with our group – the General, De Griers, Mademoiselle Blanche and the mother. Polina and Mr Astley weren't there, though.

'Well, well, well!' exclaimed Grandmother. 'But we've no time to stop. What do you want? I can't talk to you now!'

I dropped behind a little, and immediately was pounced on by De Griers.

'She's lost this morning's winnings,' I whispered, 'and another twelve thousand gulden besides. Right now we're on our way to get some bonds changed.'

De Griers stamped his foot with vexation, and hurried to communicate the news to the General.

Meanwhile we continued to wheel the old lady along.

'Stop her, stop her,' whispered the General in consternation.

'Maybe you should try and stop her yourself,' I whispered back.

'My dear Aunt,' he said as he approached her, 'Auntie, we were just . . .' (his voice was beginning to tremble and falter) ' . . . we've hired a horse for a drive out of town. There's an enchanting view not far from here. We – we – we were just coming to invite you to join us.'

'To hang with you and your views!' said Grandmother angrily, waving him away.

'And there are trees there, and we could have tea under them,' continued the General, now in utter despair.

'Nous boirons du lait, sur l'herbe fraîche,'[40] added De Griers with the snarl almost of a wild beast. (This "du lait, de l'herbe fraîche" is the idyll of the Parisian bourgeoisie, their conception of "la nature et la verité"[41]!)

'Away with you and your milk!' shouted the old lady. 'You go and stuff yourself as much as you like, but my stomach simply recoils from the very idea. What are you holding me up for, anyway? I've nothing to say to you.'

'Here we are, Grandmother,' I announced. 'Here's the money-changer's office.'

I went in to get the securities changed, while Grandmother remained outside in the porch, and the rest waited a little distance away, in doubt as to their best course of action. Eventually the old lady glared at them so angrily that they went off along the road towards the casino.

The rate of exchange was so bad that I refused to accept it and went back out to Grandmother for instructions.

'The robbers!' she exclaimed, flinging her hands in the air. 'Never mind, though. Get the documents cashed. No, send the banker out to me,' she added as an afterthought.

'Would one of the clerks do, Grandmother?'

'Yes, one of the clerks. It's all one. The robbers!'

The clerk consented to come out when he saw that he was being asked for by an elderly countess who was too weak to walk, after which Grandmother upbraided him at length, and with great vehemence, for his alleged usury, and to bargain with him in a mixture of Russian, French and German – with me acting as interpreter. All the while, the grave-faced official eyed us both and silently shook his head. At

Grandmother, in particular, he gazed with a curiosity which almost bordered on rudeness. At length, he began to smile.

'Mind your manners!' cried the old lady. 'And may my money choke you! Alexei Ivanovich, tell him we can easily try someone else.'

'The clerk says that the others would give you even less than he's offering.'

What the final rate of exchange he offered was, I don't exactly remember, but at all events the results were alarming. I got twelve thousand florins in gold, and the receipt, which I took out to Grandmother.

'Oh, I'm no accountant,' she said, waving the piece of paper aside. 'Let's hurry back, let's just hurry back. But I don't mean to wager a penny on that blasted zero, nor on the equally damned red,' she muttered to herself as we entered the casino.

This time I did all I could to persuade the old lady to stake as little as possible, saying that a time would come when she would be at liberty to wager more with a better chance of success. But she was so impatient that, though at first she agreed to do as I suggested, nothing could stop her when once she had begun. As soon as she started, she won bets of a hundred and two hundred gulden. 'There you are!' she said, prodding me. 'See what we've won! Surely it would be worth our while to stake four thousand now instead of a hundred, because we might win another four thousand, and then . . . Oh, it was *your* fault before, all your fault!'

I felt greatly put out as I watched her play, but I decided to hold my tongue and give her no more advice.

Suddenly De Griers appeared on the scene. It seems that all this while he and the others had been standing near us, though I noticed that Mademoiselle Blanche had withdrawn a little from the rest, and was flirting with the Prince. Clearly the General was greatly put out at this. Indeed, he was in a perfect agony of vexation. But Mademoiselle was careful never to look his way, though he did his best to attract her attention. The poor General! By turns his face went white and then red, and he was trembling to such an extent he could scarcely follow

the old lady's play. At length Mademoiselle and the Prince left, and
the General followed them.

'Madame, Madame,' said De Griers in honeyed tones as he leant
over to whisper in Grandmother's ear. 'That bet will never win. No,
no, it's impossible,' he added in broken Russian. 'No, no!'

'But why not?' asked Grandmother, turning round. 'Show me what
I ought to do.'

Instantly De Griers burst into a babble of French as he offered
advice, fussed about, declared that we ought to be wait for this or that
chance, and started to calculate odds. All this advice he addressed to
me in my capacity as translator, while tapping the table with his finger,
and pointing here and there. At length he seized a pencil and began
to make calculations on paper until he had exhausted Grandmother's
patience.

'Oh, away with you!' she interrupted him. 'You're talking sheer
nonsense, because, although you keep saying "Madame, this, Madame,
that", you haven't the slightest idea what ought to be done. Just go
away, I tell you!'

'But, Madame,' cooed De Griers, and straightaway started over again
with his fussy instructions.

'Wager just *once* as he advises,' Grandmother said to me, 'and then
we will see what we will see. Of course, his bet *might* win.'

As a matter of fact, De Grier's one object was to distract the old
lady from staking large sums, for which reason he now suggested
to her that she should bet on certain numbers, singly and in groups.
Consequently, in accordance with his instructions, I staked a gold
friedrich on each of the odd numbers between one and twelve and
five friedrichs on the groups of numbers from twelve to eighteen
and from eighteen to twenty-four. The total stake amounted to 160
gulden.

The wheel revolved. 'Zero!' cried the croupier.

We'd lost it all!

'You fool!' shouted the old lady, turning on De Griers. 'You damned
Frenchman, to think that you should advise me what to do! Leave us

alone! You make such a fuss, but you haven't a clue what you're talking about.'

Deeply offended, De Griers shrugged his shoulders, favoured Grandmother with a look of contempt, and walked off. For some time he had been feeling ashamed of being seen in such company, and this was the last straw.

An hour later we'd lost everything we had.

'Home!' shouted Grandmother.

Not until we had turned into the avenue did she utter another word, but from that point onwards, until we arrived at the hotel, she kept exclaiming 'What a fool I am! What a silly old fool I am, to be sure!'

Arrived at the hotel, she called for tea, and then gave orders for her luggage to be packed.

'We're off again,' she announced.

'But where to, Madame?' inquired Marfa.

'What's that to do with *you*? Mind your own business. Potapych, have everything packed, we're returning to Moscow at once. I've just squandered fifteen thousand roubles.'

'Fifteen thousand roubles, Mistress? My God!' And Potapych spat on his hands, probably to show that he was ready to serve her in any way he could.

'Now then, you fool! Don't start weeping and wailing! Just be quiet, and get everything ready. And run downstairs and get my hotel bill.'

'The next train leaves at 9:30, Grandmother,' I interposed, with a view to controlling her agitation.

'And what's the time now?'

'Half past seven.'

'How annoying! But never mind. Alexei Ivanovich, I haven't a kopeck on me now. I have nothing but these two banknotes. Run to the office and get them changed. Otherwise I will have nothing to travel with.'

I set off on her errand, and returned half an hour later to find the whole party gathered in her rooms. It appeared that the news of her impending departure for Moscow had thrown the conspirators into a consternation even greater than her losses had done. For, said they, even if her departure should save her fortune, what will become of the General later? Who was to repay De Griers? Clearly Mademoiselle Blanche would never consent to wait until Grandmother was dead, but would at once elope with the Prince or someone else. So they were all there, endeavouring to calm Grandmother down and change her mind. Only Polina was missing. For her part, Grandmother had nothing for the party but abuse.

'Away with you all, you rascals!' she was shouting. 'What have my affairs to do with you? Why, in particular, have *you*' – here she indicated De Griers – 'come sneaking around here with your goaty beard? And what do *you* want?' – here she turned to Mademoiselle Blanche – 'What are *you* trying to wheedle out of me?'

'Diantre!'[42] muttered Mademoiselle under her breath, but her eyes were flashing. Then all at once she burst out laughing and left the room, shouting to the General as she did so: 'Elle vivra cent ans!'[43]

'So you've all been counting on my death, have you?' raged the old lady. 'Away with you! Clear them out of the room, Alexei Ivanovich. What business is it of *theirs*? It's not *their* money I've been squandering, but mine, my own.'

The General shrugged his shoulders, bowed and withdrew, with De Griers behind him.

'Call Praskovya,' commanded Grandmother, and in five minutes Marfa reappeared with Polina, who had been sitting with the children in her own room (having deliberately decided not to come out that day). Her face looked grave and careworn.

'Praskovya,' began Grandmother, 'is what I have just learned by accident true? Is that fool of a stepfather of yours going to marry that silly whirligig of a Frenchwoman – that actress, or something worse? Tell me, is it true?'

'I don't know *for certain*, Grandmother,' replied Polina, 'but from Mademoiselle Blanche's account – because she doesn't appear to think it necessary to conceal anything – I conclude that . . .'

'You need say no more,' interrupted Grandmother animatedly. 'I understand the situation. I always thought he would do something like this, because I always looked on him as a useless, frivolous person who gave himself ridiculous airs because of his being a general – though he only got that rank because he retired as a colonel. Yes, I know all about the sending of the telegrams to inquire whether "the old woman is likely to turn up her toes soon". Ah, so they were looking for the legacies! Without the money that wretched woman – what's her name? Oh, yes, De Cominges – would never dream of accepting the General and his false teeth – no, not even as her servant – since she herself, so they say, has a pile of money and lends it on interest, and makes a good thing out of it too. However, it's not you, Praskovya, that I blame; it wasn't you who sent those telegrams. Nor, for that matter, do I wish to talk about the past. True, I know that you're a vixen by nature, a wasp that will sting anyone who touches it, but my heart grieves for you, because I loved your mother, Katerina. Now, will you give up everything here and come away with me? Otherwise, I don't know what is to become of you, and it's not right that you should continue to live with these people. Wait,' she interposed as Polina attempted to speak, 'I've not finished yet. I ask nothing of you in return. My house in Moscow is, as you know, large enough to be a palace, and you could occupy a whole floor of it if you liked and keep away from me for weeks on end. Will you come with me or won't you?'

'First of all, let me ask *you*,' replied Polina, 'whether you're really intending to leave at once?'

'What? Do you think I'm joking? I've said I'm going, and I *am* going. Today I've squandered fifteen thousand roubles at that damned roulette of yours, and though, five years ago, I promised the people of a certain suburb of Moscow to build them a stone church in place of a wooden one, I have frittered away my money here! However, I'm now going back to build my church.'

'But what about the waters, Grandmother? Surely you came here to take the waters?'

'Who cares about your stupid waters! Don't make me angry,

Praskovya. Is that what you're trying to do? Tell me, then: will you or won't you come with me?'

'Grandmother,' Polina replied with deep feeling, 'I'm very, very grateful to you for the shelter you've so kindly offered me. Also, to a certain extent you have guessed my position correctly, and I am beholden to you to such an extent that it may be that I will come and live with you, very soon. But there are important reasons why . . . why I can't decide just yet. If you would let me have, say, a couple of weeks to make up my mind?'

'You mean you're *not* coming?'

'All I mean is that I can't come just yet. At all events, I couldn't very well leave my little brother and sister here since, if I were to leave them, they would be completely abandoned. But if, Grandmother, you would take the little ones *and* me, then, of course, I could come with you and would do all I could to serve you' (this she said with great earnestness). 'Only, without the little ones, I *can't* come.'

'Don't whine!' (As a matter of fact, Polina never ever whined or cried). 'We can find a place for your chickens; it's a big henhouse. In any case, it's time they went to school. Do you still not want to come? Look here, Praskovya. I wish you well, and nothing but well, but I've guessed the real reason why you won't come. Yes, I know all about it, Praskovya. That Frenchman will never bring you good of any sort.'

Polina flushed, and I jumped. 'Everyone seems to know about this affair. Maybe I'm the only one who didn't know about it!' I thought to myself.

'Now, now! Don't scowl,' continued Grandmother. 'I don't want to make an issue of this. Just take care that no harm comes to you, won't you? For you're a sensible girl, and I would be sorry for you – I regard you in a different light to the rest of them. And now, please, leave me. Goodbye.'

'But let me see you off,' said Polina.

'No, you needn't. Don't make a fuss. You and all the rest of them have tired me out.'

But when Polina tried to kiss Grandmother's hand, the old lady withdrew it and kissed the girl on the cheek. As she passed me, Polina gave me a quick glance, and then as swiftly averted her eyes.

'And goodbye to you too, Alexei Ivanovich. The train leaves in an hour's time, and I think you must be weary of me. Take these five hundred gulden for yourself.'

'I thank you humbly, Grandmother, but I would be ashamed to . . .'

'Come on, come on!' exclaimed Grandmother so forcefully, and with such an air of menace, that I didn't dare refuse the money.

'If, when in Moscow, you have no place to lay your head,' she added, 'come and see me, and I will give you a recommendation. Now, Potapych, get our things ready.'

I went up to my room, and lay down on the bed. I must have lain like that for a whole hour, with my head resting on my hand. So the crisis had come! I needed time to think about that. Tomorrow I would have a talk with Polina. Ah! The Frenchman! So it was true? But how could it be? Polina and De Griers! What a combination!

No, it was too improbable. Suddenly I jumped up with the idea of looking for Astley and making him tell me. There could be no doubt that he knew more than I did. Astley? Well, he was another problem for me to solve.

Suddenly there was a knock at the door, and I opened it to find Potapych standing there.

'Sir,' he said, 'my mistress is asking for you.'

'Indeed? But she's just leaving, isn't she? The train leaves in ten minutes' time.'

'She's anxious, sir. She cannot rest. She keeps saying, "Hurry, Hurry." She means she wants you, sir. For the love of God, come quickly, sir, without delay.'

I ran downstairs at once. Grandmother was just being carried out of her rooms into the corridor. In her hands she held a roll of banknotes.

'Alexei Ivanovich,' she cried, 'you lead the way, we're off again.'

'But where to, Grandmother?'

'I cannot rest until I have made good my losses. You walk on ahead. No questions! Play continues until midnight, does it not?'

For a moment I stood stupefied, deep in thought, but it was not long before I made up my mind.

'With your permission, Grandmother,' I said, 'I won't go with you.'

'And why not? What do you mean? Has everyone here gone mad?'

'I beg your forgiveness, but I want to have nothing to reproach myself with later. So I won't go with you. I intend neither to watch you play nor to participate. I also wish to return your five hundred gulden. Goodbye.'

Laying the money on a little table which happened to be beside Grandmother's chair, I bowed and withdrew.

'What nonsense!' Grandmother shouted after me. 'Very well, then. Don't come, I'll find my own way. Potapych, you must come with me. Well, lift up the chair, carry me!'

I failed to find Mr Astley, and returned home. Later, sometime after midnight, I learned from Potapych how Grandmother's day had ended. She had lost all the money which, earlier in the day, I had got for her paper securities, a sum amounting to about ten thousand roubles. This she did under the direction of the Pole to whom, that afternoon, she had handed over two gold friedrichs. Before his arrival on the scene, she had ordered Potapych to bet for her, but eventually she had told him to go away, at which point the Pole had leapt into the breach. Not only did he know some Russian, but he could speak three languages, so the pair of them were able to understand one another well enough. The old lady was rude to him all the time despite his deferential manner, and compared him unfavourably with myself (at least, so Potapych said). 'You,' the old chamberlain said to me, 'treated her as a gentleman should, but him, he robbed her right, left and centre, as I saw with my own eyes. Twice she caught him at it, and berated him soundly. On one occasion she even pulled his hair, which made the bystanders laugh. But she lost everything, sir, that is to say, she lost all the money you got for her at the money-changers. Then we brought her home, and, after asking for some water and saying her prayers, she went to bed. So worn out she was that she fell asleep at once. May God send her dreams of angels! And this is all this foreign travel has done for us! Oh, to be in Moscow! Is there anything we haven't got at home there, in Moscow? Such a garden and flowers as you could never see here, and fresh air and apple-trees coming into blossom, and a beautiful view to look at. Oh, why did she have to go travelling abroad? Oh dear, oh dear, oh dear!'

XIII

Almost a month has passed since I last touched these notes, notes which I began under the influence of impressions at once intense and confused. The catastrophe which I then felt to be approaching has now arrived, but in a form a hundred times more dramatic and unexpected than I had envisaged. To me it all seems strange, shocking, even tragic. Certain things happened to me that bordered on the miraculous. At all events, that's how I still see them now, though considering the maelstrom of events I was caught up in at the time, they were perhaps only slightly out of the ordinary. But the most curious thing of all is my attitude to those events. Even now I still don't understand myself. But it has all faded away like a dream. Even my passion for Polina is dead, and that was certainly strong and sincere. So what has become of it now? At times I fancy that I must have been mad, that I was sitting in a madhouse, that these events merely *seemed* to happen; that they still merely seem to be happening.

I've been sorting and re-reading my notes (perhaps to convince myself that I'm not in a madhouse). At present, I'm lonely and all alone. Autumn is coming; the leaves are already turning yellow. And as I sit brooding in this depressing little town (and oh, how depressing little German towns can be!), I find myself taking no thought for the future, but living under the influence of passing moods and of my recollections of the storm which recently dragged me into a whirlwind and then threw me out again. At times, I still seem to be caught up in that whirlwind. At times, it seems that the storm is gathering once again, and that as it passes overhead, it will gather me in until I have lost any sense of order and reality, and will just go on spinning and spinning and spinning . . .

Yet it may be that I'll be able to stop myself spinning if I can just manage to provide myself with an exact account of what has happened over the past month. Somehow I feel drawn towards my pen again; on many an evening I have nothing else in the world to do but write,

although, curiously enough, of late I have taken to amusing myself
with the works of Paul de Kock[44], which I read in German translations
I got from the wretched local library. I really can't abide these books,
but I still read them, and find myself amazed that I should be doing
so. Somehow I seem to be afraid of any *serious* book, afraid of permitting any *serious* preoccupation to break the spell of the passing moment.
It's as if this formless dream I have been speaking about, and the
impressions it has left behind, are so dear to me that I fear to disturb
the vision with anything new, lest it should dissolve in smoke. But is
the dream so dear to me? Yes, it *is* dear to me, and will ever be fresh
in my memory, even forty years from now . . .

So let me write about it, even if only in part and in a more abridged
form than my full impressions might warrant.

First of all, let me finish Grandmother's story. The next day she lost
every single gulden she possessed. It was bound to happen like that,
for people like her, once they have started on that path, slip down it
faster and faster, just like a sledge sliding down a snowy hillside. She
played the whole day until eight o'clock that evening, and though I
personally did not witness her exploits, I was told what happened later.

All that day Potapych remained in attendance on her, but the Poles
who were directing her betting changed more than once. To start with,
she dismissed the Pole who had played for her the previous day, the
one whose hair she had pulled, and took on another one; but he proved
even worse than the one before, and was dismissed in favour of the
first Pole again, who, during the time of his unemployment, had nevertheless continued to hover round Grandmother's chair, and from time
to time stuck his head over her shoulder. Eventually the old lady was
in despair, because the second Pole, when dismissed, imitated his
predecessor by refusing to go away, with the result that there was one
Pole standing to the right of their victim and the other on her left,
from which vantage points the two of them quarrelled, insulted each
other over the bets they were placing, and called each other 'laidak'
(that's Polish for 'rogue') and other similar terms of endearment.
Finally, they had a mutual reconciliation, and, tossing the money around

any old how, simply played at random. Quarrelling once more, each of them staked money on his own side of Grandmother's chair (for instance, the one Pole wagered on red, and the other one on black), until they had so confused and demoralised the old lady that, nearly in tears, she was forced to appeal to the head croupier for protection and have the two Poles thrown out. No time was lost in this being done, despite the rascals' cries and protestations that the old lady was in their debt, that she had cheated them and that her general behaviour had been mean and dishonourable. The same evening the unfortunate Potapych related the story to me with tears in his eyes, complaining that the two men had stuffed their pockets with money (he himself had seen them do it) which had been shamelessly stolen from his mistress. For instance, one Pole demanded fifty gulden from Grandmother for his trouble, and then staked the money beside her stake. She happened to win, at which he shouted out that the winning stake was his and that she had lost. As soon as the two Poles had been thrown out, Potapych left the room, and reported to the authorities that the men's pockets were full of her money; and, on Grandmother also asking the head croupier to look into the affair, the police made their appearance and, despite the protests of the Poles (who, indeed, had been caught red-handed), their pockets were turned inside out and the contents handed back to Grandmother. In fact, in view of the fact that she had lost all day, the croupiers and the casino authorities showed her every consideration and her fame spread through the town; visitors of every nationality, humble and distinguished alike, crowded in to get a glimpse of 'la vieille comtesse russe, tombée en enfance'[45] who had lost 'several million'.

With the money the authorities restored to her from the pockets of the Poles Grandmother achieved very, very little, for there soon arrived to take his countrymen's place a third Pole, a man who could speak Russian fluently, who was dressed like a gentleman (albeit in a rather flunkeyish style) and who sported a huge moustache. Though polite enough to the old lady, he was rather haughty to the bystanders and was quite despotic with regard to the betting. In short, he offered himself to Grandmother less as a servant than as her master. After each round he would turn to the old lady and swear terrible oaths to the effect that he was a 'Polish gentleman of honour' who would scorn to take a kopeck of her money. He repeated these oaths so often that she began to feel alarmed, but since he was improving her betting and had begun to win on her behalf, she felt that she couldn't very well get rid of him. An hour later, the two Poles who earlier in the day had been thrown out of the casino, made a reappearance behind the old lady's chair and renewed their offers of service, even if only to be sent on errands; but Potapych told me that these rascals exchanged winks with the said 'gentleman of honour', and the latter handed something to them. Next, since Grandmother had not yet had lunch – she had scarcely left her chair for a moment – one of the two Poles ran to the casino restaurant and brought her a bowl of soup, and afterwards some tea. In fact, *both* Poles hastened to run errands for her. Eventually, at the end of the day, when it was clear that Grandmother was about to lose her very last coin, standing behind her chair were no fewer than six natives of Poland who had never been seen or heard before; and as soon as the old lady staked the coin in question, they took no further notice of her, but pushed their way past her chair to the table, grabbed the money and staked it, shouting and arguing all the while, and squabbling with the 'gentleman of honour' (who also had forgotten Grandmother's existence) as though he was their equal. Even when Grandmother had lost everything, and was returning (about eight o'clock) to the hotel, some three or four Poles could not bring themselves to leave her, but continued running beside her chair and protesting volubly that Grandmother had cheated them and that she ought to be made to hand over what was not hers. Thus the party arrived at the hotel, from which the rogues were soon unceremoniously ejected.

According to Potapych's calculations, Grandmother lost, that day, a total of ninety thousand roubles, in addition to the money she had lost the day before. All the paper securities she had brought with her – the five per cent bonds, the loan scrips, her shares – she had converted into cash. I couldn't help but marvel at the way in which, for seven or eight hours at a stretch, she had sat in that chair of hers, almost never leaving the table. Potapych told me that there were three occasions on which she had really began to win, but that, led on by false hopes, she was unable to tear herself away at the right moment. Every gambler knows that a person may sit for a day and a night playing cards without ever looking to right or to left.

Meanwhile, some other very important events were taking place in our hotel that day. As early as eleven o'clock – that is to say, before Grandmother had left her rooms – the General and De Griers decided on their final ploy: on learning that the old lady had changed her mind about leaving and was set on heading for the casino again, the whole group (except for Polina) proceeded en masse to her rooms, for the purpose of finally and frankly talking things over with her. But the General, quaking in his shoes and extremely worried about his possible future, overdid it. After half an hour of prayers and entreaties, along with a full admission of his debts, and even of his passion for Mademoiselle Blanche (yes, he had completely lost his head), he suddenly adopted a threatening tone and started to rage at the old lady, shouting that she was sullying the family honour, that she was making a public scandal of herself, and that she was bringing shame on the fair name of Russia itself, which could be a matter for the police. The upshot was that Grandmother chased him out of the room with her stick (yes, with a real stick!). Later in the morning he consulted De Griers several times, the question which occupied him being: was there any way they could involve the police, to tell them that 'this respected, but unfortunate, old lady has gone out of her mind, and is squandering her last kopeck', or something like that? In short, was it in any way possible to engineer some sort of supervision over, or restraint on, the old lady? De Griers, however, shrugged his shoulders at this, and laughed in the General's face, while the old warrior went on talking volubly and striding up and down his study. Finally De Griers went off with a dismissive wave of his hand, and by the evening we learned that he had left the hotel, after having a very secret and important discussion with Mademoiselle Blanche. As for the latter, she too had

taken decisive steps from early morning; she completely excluded the
General from her presence, bestowing not even a glance on him. Indeed,
even when the General pursued her to the casino, and met her walking
arm in arm with the Prince, he (the General) received from her and
her mother not the slightest sign of recognition. Nor did the Prince
himself bow. The rest of the day Mademoiselle spent probing the
Prince, trying to make him declare himself, but she then found she
had made a terrible mistake. This minor tragedy occurred that evening.
Mademoiselle Blanche suddenly discovered that the Prince had not a
penny to his name, but, on the contrary, had been intending to borrow
money from her to play roulette. In high dudgeon she chased him away
and shut herself in her room.

That same morning I went to see – or, rather, spent some time
looking for – Mr Astley, but was unsuccessful in my quest. He was
nowhere to be found, neither in his rooms nor in the casino nor in the
park; nor, that day, did he lunch at his hotel as usual. However, at
about five o'clock I caught sight of him walking from the railway
station to the Hôtel d'Angleterre. He seemed to be in a great hurry
and deep in thought, though in his face I could discern no actual traces
of worry or agitation. He cordially held out his hand to me, with his
usual exclamation of 'Ah!' but didn't slow down. I turned and walked
beside him, but found, somehow, that his answers didn't give me any
definite information. Moreover, I felt reluctant to speak to him about
Polina, nor, for his part, did he ask me any questions about her, although,
on my telling him of Grandmother's exploits, he listened attentively
and gravely, and then shrugged his shoulders.

'She's gambling away everything she has,' I remarked.

'Oh yes. She arrived at the casino even before I left, and I knew
she would lose. If I have time, I'll go to the casino tonight and see
what's happening. It's a strange business.'

'Where have you been today?' I asked, surprised at myself for not
yet having asked the question.

'In Frankfurt.'

'On business?'

'Yes, on business.'

What more could I ask after that? I accompanied him until, as we drew level with the Hôtel des Quatre Saisons, he suddenly nodded to me and disappeared. For my part, I went back home. I came to the conclusion that, even if I'd talked to him for two hours, I would have learnt nothing more from him because I had no definite questions to ask. It was bound to have been like that. It was quite impossible for me to formulate the question I really wanted to ask.

Polina spent the whole of that day either walking round the park with the nurse and children or sitting in her own room. She'd been avoiding the General for some time and had scarcely said a word to him (scarcely a word, I mean, on any *serious* matter). Yes, I'd noticed that. Still, since I was aware of the position in which the General now found himself, I didn't think he could avoid talking to *her*; there would have to be some discussion of family matters. However, when I was returning to the hotel after my conversation with Astley and chanced to meet Polina and the children, I could see that her face was quite calm; it seemed as though the family troubles were having no effect on her. She responded to my bow with only a slight nod, and I retired to my room in a very bad mood.

Of course, since the affair with the Burmerhelms I had been avoiding Polina and had exchanged not a word with her. But this was just a front, and as time went on, there arose in me an ever-increasing indignation. Even if she didn't love me she shouldn't trample on my feelings like that or accept my confessions of love with such indifference. After all, she was aware that I loved her (she had freely allowed me to tell her so). Of course, our relationship had arisen in a strange way. About two months ago, I had noticed that she wanted to make me her friend, her confidant, that she was testing me for that purpose; but for some reason or another, the desired result had never come about, and we had fallen into our present strange relationship, which was what had led me to speak to her as I had done. At the same time, if my love was distasteful to her, why had she not forbidden me to speak to her about it?

But she had not forbidden me to do so. On the contrary, there had been occasions when she had even *invited* me to speak of it. Of course, this might have been done out of sheer wantonness, for I well knew – I had noticed it only too often – that, after listening to what I had to say and exasperating me almost beyond endurance, she loved to suddenly torture me with some fresh outburst of contempt and indifference! Yet she must know that I can't live without her. Three days had elapsed since the business with the Baron, and I could bear the separation no longer. When, earlier that afternoon, I met her near the casino, my heart had beaten so violently that I almost fainted. And she can't live without me either. Didn't she say she needed me? Or had that, too, just been said as a joke?

She had a secret of some kind, there could be no doubt about that. What she had said to Grandmother had stabbed me to the heart. On a thousand occasions I had challenged her to be frank with me, and she knew I was ready to give my very life for her. Yet she had always kept me at a distance with that contemptuous air of hers, or else she had demanded of me, in lieu of the life which I offered to lay at her feet, such escapades as I had perpetrated with the Baron. Ah, was it not torture to me, all this? For could it be that her whole world was bound up with the Frenchman? And what about Mr Astley? The whole business was beyond me. My God, how it was torturing me!

Having arrived home, in a fit of frenzy I grabbed a pen and scribbled the following note to her:

'Polina Alexandrovna, I can see that matters are coming to a head and that they will involve you too. For the last time I ask you, do you, or do you not, need my life? If you do, then I'm at your disposal. I'll be in my room. If you have need of my life, write or send for me.'

I sealed the letter, and gave it to one of the hotel footmen to deliver, with orders to hand it to the addressee in person. I didn't expect an answer, but scarcely three minutes had passed before the fellow returned with 'the compliments of a certain person'.

About seven o'clock, I was sent for by the General. I found him in his study, apparently preparing to go out again, as his hat and stick were lying on the sofa. When I entered, he was standing in the middle of the room with his feet apart and his head drooping. He seemed to be talking to himself. But as soon as he saw me at the door he came towards me in such a strange way that I involuntarily took a step back and was about to leave when he seized me by both hands and, pulling me towards the sofa and seating himself on it, he made me sit on a chair opposite him. Then, without letting go of my hands, he exclaimed with trembling lips and a sparkle of tears in his eyes:

'Oh, Alexei Ivanovich! Save me, save me! Have mercy on me!'

For a long time I couldn't make out what he meant, though he kept on talking and talking, and constantly repeating 'Have mercy, have mercy!' Eventually, however, I guessed that he was looking to me to give him some advice, or else that, abandoned by everyone and over-whelmed by grief and apprehension, he had remembered my existence and sent for me to relieve his feelings by just talking and talking and talking.

In fact, he was in such a confused and despondent state of mind that, clasping his hands together, he actually went down on his knees and begged me to go to Mademoiselle Blanche, and beg and advise her to return to him and accept him in marriage.

'But, General,' I exclaimed, 'Mademoiselle Blanche has scarcely even noticed my existence. What could I possibly do?'

My protests were in vain, he couldn't understand anything that was being said to him. Next he started talking about Grandmother, but totally incoherently, his one thought being to send for the police.

'In Russia,' he said, suddenly boiling over with indignation, 'or in any well-ordered state where there exists a government, old women like my aunt are placed under proper guardianship. Yes, my good sir,' he went on, relapsing into a reproving tone as he leapt to his feet and started to pace up and down the room, 'do you not know this,' (he seemed to be addressing some imaginary listener in the corner) 'do you not know that in Russia old women like her are kept under control, under control, yes, under control, damn it?'

He flung himself back down on the sofa. A minute later, though

sobbing and almost gasping for breath, he managed to tell me that
Mademoiselle Blanche had refused to marry him because Grandmother
had turned up instead of a telegram and it was therefore clear that he
had no inheritance coming to him. Evidently he supposed that I had
up till then been entirely ignorant of all this. Again, when I referred
to De Griers, the General made a gesture of despair. 'He's gone away,'
he said, 'and everything I own is mortgaged to him. I stand here
stripped to my bare skin. Even of the money you brought me from
Paris, I don't know if there is more than seven hundred francs left. Of
course, that amount will do to be going on with, but, as regards the
future, I don't know, I just don't know.'

'Then how will you pay your hotel bill?' I exclaimed in alarm. 'And
what will you do after that?'

He looked at me pensively, but it was clear he hadn't understood
– perhaps hadn't even heard – what I'd said. Then I tried to get him
to talk about Polina and the children, but he only returned brief answers
of 'Yes, yes' and again started to maunder on about the Prince and the
likelihood of the latter marrying Mademoiselle Blanche. 'What on
earth am I to do?' he concluded. 'What on earth am I to do? Is this
not ingratitude? Is it not sheer ingratitude?' And he burst into tears.

Nothing could be done with such a man. But it was dangerous to
leave him alone, something might happen to him. I managed to get
away, but I warned the nanny to keep an eye on him, and had a word
with the footman in the corridor (a very sensible fellow), who likewise
promised to watch him.

I had hardly left the General when Potapych approached me with
a summons from Grandmother. It was now eight o'clock, and she had
returned from the casino after finally losing everything she had. I found
her sitting in her chair, very distressed and clearly exhausted. Presently
Marfa brought her up a cup of tea and made her drink it; yet even
then I could detect a great change in the old lady's tone and manner.

'Good evening, Alexei Ivanovich, my good fellow,' she said slowly,
her head drooping. 'Pardon me for disturbing you again. Yes, you must
pardon an old woman like me. Do you know what I've done, my

friend? I've left behind me all I possess, nearly a hundred thousand roubles! You were quite right to refuse to come with me this evening. Now I have no money, not a kopeck. But I mustn't delay, I must leave by the 9:30 train. I've sent for that English friend of yours, and I'm going to beg him to lend me three thousand francs for a week. Please try to persuade him not to refuse me, because I'm still a rich woman who owns three villages and a couple of mansions. The money will be found, I've not yet squandered *everything*. I'm telling you this so that he may have no doubts about . . . Ah, but here he is! Clearly he's a good man.'

Sure enough, Astley had come hot-foot on receiving Grandmother's appeal. Scarcely stopping even to think, and with scarcely a word, he counted out the three thousand francs against a note of hand which she duly signed. Then, his business done, he bowed and lost no time in taking his leave of us.

'You go, too, Alexei Ivanovich,' said Grandmother. 'My bones are aching, and I still have an hour in which I can have a rest. Don't be hard on me, old fool that I am. Never again will I blame young people for being frivolous. I would think it wrong of me even to blame that unhappy General of yours. Nevertheless, I don't mean to let him have any of my money, which is all he wants, because I consider him a perfect fool, even though I've no more sense than he has. How surely does God visit afflictions on old age and punish it for its presumption! Well, goodbye. Marfa, come and lift me up.'

Nevertheless, I had a mind to see the old lady off. Moreover, I was in a state of suspense; somehow, I kept thinking, *something* was going to happen. I couldn't stay quietly in my room. I stepped out into the corridor and then into the chestnut avenue for a few minutes' stroll. My letter to Polina had been clear and firm, and the present crisis, I felt sure, would prove conclusive. I had heard of De Griers' departure, and, however much Polina might reject me as a *friend*, she might not reject me altogether as a *servant*. She would need me to fetch and carry for her, and I was ready to do so. How could it be otherwise?

Towards the time of the train's departure I hurried to the station and put Grandmother into her compartment. She and her party were occupying a reserved family carriage.

'Thank you for your unselfish help,' she said as we parted. 'Oh, and please remind Praskovya what I said to her last night. I expect to see her soon.'

Then I returned home. As I was passing the door of the General's suite, I met the nanny and asked after her master. 'There's nothing new to report, sir,' she replied quietly. Nevertheless I decided to go in, and was just doing so when I stopped thunderstruck on the threshold. For before me I saw the General and Mademoiselle Blanche – laughing merrily with one another! – while beside them, on the sofa, was seated her mother. Clearly the General was almost delirious with joy, as he was talking all sorts of nonsense and breaking out into gusts of nervous laughter which twisted his face into innumerable wrinkles that made his eyes almost disappear.

Afterwards I learnt from Mademoiselle Blanche herself that, after dismissing the Prince and hearing of the General's tears, she decided to go and comfort the old man, and had just come for that purpose when I arrived. Fortunately, the poor General didn't know that his fate had already been decided, that Mademoiselle had been packing her trunks in readiness for leaving on the first train in the morning to Paris!

Hesitating a moment at the doorway I changed my mind about going in and left unnoticed. Going up to my own room, on opening the door I made out in the semi-darkness a figure seated on a chair in the corner by the window. The figure did not get up when I went in, so I quickly walked over to it, peered at it closely and felt my heart almost stop beating. It was Polina!

XIV

I shouted out in my surprise.

'What's the matter? What's the matter?' she asked in a strange voice. She was looking pale, and her eyes were sombre.

'What do you mean, what's the matter? You, you're here, in my room!'

'If I come, then *all* of me comes,' she said. 'That has always been my way, as you will see in a moment. Please light a candle.'

I did so. She stood up, went over to the table, and laid down an open letter.

'Read it,' she said.

'It is De Griers' handwriting!' I exclaimed as I seized the document. My hands were trembling so much that the lines on the pages were dancing before my eyes. Although, at this distance of time, I have forgotten the exact wording of the letter, what follows will give you the general sense of what was written:

'Mademoiselle,' De Griers had written, 'certain untoward circumstances compel me to depart in haste. Of course, you yourself will have noticed that I have refrained from giving you any final explanation until the whole situation became clear. Now the arrival of the old lady and her subsequent behaviour have put an end to my uncertainty. The complicated state of my affairs forbids me to continue to nourish those hopes of ultimate bliss upon which, for a long while past, I have permitted myself to feed. I regret the past, but at the same time hope that in my conduct you have never been able to detect anything that was unworthy of a gentleman and a man of honour. However, having lost almost all my money in loans to your stepfather, I find myself driven by the necessity of saving the remainder. I have therefore instructed certain friends of mine in St Petersburg to arrange for the sale of all the property that has been mortgaged to me. At the same time, knowing that your frivolous stepfather has squandered money which is exclusively yours, I have decided to absolve him from fifty thousand francs' worth of debt, in order that you may be in a position to recover from him what you have lost by suing him in the law courts. I trust, therefore, that, as matters now stand, this action of mine may bring you some benefit. I trust also that this same action leaves me in the position of having fulfilled every obligation which is incumbent upon a man of honour and refinement. Rest assured that your memory will for ever remain graven in my heart.'

'That's all clear enough,' I said, adding indignantly, 'Surely you didn't expect anything else from him?'

'I expected nothing at all from him,' she replied, calmly enough, it seemed, but with a tremor in her voice. 'I made up my mind on that subject long ago, because I could read his mind and knew what he was thinking. He thought that I might possibly sue him, that one day I might become a nuisance.' Here Polina stopped for a moment, and stood biting her lips. 'So I deliberately redoubled my contemptuous treatment of him, and waited to see what he would do. If a telegram had arrived from St Petersburg to say that we were inheriting the money, I would have flung at him a note of hand for my foolish step-father's debts and then sent him packing. I've hated him for a long time now. He was a different man before, but now, now he's . . . Oh, how glad I would be to throw that fifty thousand in his face and spit at him . . . and rub the spittle in!'

'But the document for the fifty-thousand mortgage that he returned is with the General, isn't it? If so, go and get it and send that to De Griers.'

'No, that's not the same, it's not the same!'

'Yes, you're right, it's not the same. But what can the General do now?'

Then an idea suddenly occurred to me. 'What about Grandmother?' I asked.

Polina looked at me with impatience and bewilderment.

'Why Grandmother?' she asked irritably. 'I can't go and live with her. Nor,' she added hotly, 'will I go down on my knees to beg *anyone's* pardon.'

'What's to be done, then?' I shouted. 'And how, oh how, could you ever have loved De Griers? The scoundrel, the scoundrel! But if you want, I'll kill him in a duel. Where is he now?'

'In Frankfurt, where he'll be staying for the next three days.'

'Well, just say the word, and I'll go there by the first train tomorrow,' I exclaimed with enthusiasm.

She smiled.

'If you were to do that,' she said, 'he would merely tell you to be so good as to first

give him back the fifty thousand francs. So what, then, would be the use of having a fight with him? You're talking sheer nonsense.'

'The question, then,' I went on, grinding my teeth, 'is how to raise the fifty thousand francs. We can't expect to find them just lying about on the floor. Listen. What about Mr Astley?' Even as I said that, a new and strange idea was forming itself in my brain.

Her eyes flashed.

'What? Do *you*, of all people, want me to leave you to go off with that Englishman?' she exclaimed scornfully and with a proud smile. Never before had she addressed me so intimately[46].

I think she must have become dizzy with emotion, for she suddenly sank down on the sofa, as though unable to stand any longer.

A flash of lightning seemed to strike me as I stood there. I could scarcely believe my eyes, or my ears. She *did* love me, then! It was to *me*, not to Mr Astley, that she had turned! Although she, a young girl, on her own, had come to me in my room, in a hotel, and had probably compromised herself publically by doing so, I hadn't understood!

Then a new mad idea flashed into my brain.

'Polina,' I said, 'just give me an hour. Wait here just one hour, till I get back. You must! You'll see! Just stay here, stay here!'

And I rushed out of the room without answering her look of inquiry. She shouted something after me, but I didn't turn round.

Sometimes it happens that the most insane thought, the most impossible notion, will become so fixed in one's head that at length one believes the thought or the notion to be reality. Moreover, if combined with that thought or notion there is a strong, passionate desire, one may well come to look on the said thought or notion as something inevitable, fated, foreordained – something that is bound to come to fruition. Whether in this there is also something like a build-up of anticipation, or an immense effort of will, or a feeling of intoxication caused by one's own expectations, and so on, I don't know; but at all events that night (a night I will never forget) saw something happen to me that was pretty well miraculous. Although what happened can easily be explained by arithmetic, I still believe it to have been a miracle. And why, why had this conviction gripped me so strongly and so long before then? I had indeed been thinking about it not as something that might or might not happen, but as something that was *certain* to happen.

It was a quarter past ten when I entered the casino in such a state of hope (though, at the same time, of agitation) as I had never experienced before. There were still a large number of people in the gaming-rooms, but not nearly as many as had been there in the morning.

After ten o'clock, usually the only people remaining are the real gamblers, the desperate ones, people for whom nothing exists at spas apart from roulette, and who go there for that and that alone. These gambling fanatics take little notice of what is going on around them and are interested in none of the events of the season, but play from morning till night, and would be ready to play through the night until dawn if that had been possible. As it is, they disperse reluctantly when roulette comes to an end at midnight. Likewise, as soon as the roulette is drawing to a close and the head croupier calls out 'Les trois derniers coups, messieurs'[47], most of them are ready to wager all they have in their pockets on the last three rounds – and, for the most part, lose it. For my own part, I made my way towards the table at which Grandmother had recently been sitting, and, since the crowd around it was not very large, I soon found a place where I could stand among the ring of gamblers, while directly in front of me, on the green cloth, I saw the word 'Passe'.

'Passe' is the row of numbers from 19 to 36 inclusive; the numbers from 1 to 18 inclusive is known as 'Manque'. But what had that got to do with me? I had made no calculations, I hadn't heard the numbers that had won in the last round, and made no inquiry about them when I began to play, as any *systematic* gambler would have done. No, I merely took out my store of twenty gold friedrichs, and threw them down on 'Passe', which happened to be in front of me.

'Vingt-deux!' called the croupier.

I'd won! I bet on the same again, both my original stake and my winnings.

'Trente et un!' called out the croupier.

I'd won again, and now had *eighty* gold friedrichs. Next, I moved the whole eighty on to the twelve middle numbers (a bet which, if successful, would bring me in three times the winnings, but which also involved a risk of two chances to one against). The wheel spun, and stopped at twenty-four, at which I was paid out banknotes and gold until I had by my side a total sum of two thousand gulden.

It was almost delirious as I moved the whole pile on to red. Then suddenly I came to my senses. It was the only time during the evening's play when fear cast its cold spell over me, making my hands and knees tremble. For I had realised with horror that I *had to* win, and that my whole life depended on that bet.

'Rouge!' called the croupier. I drew breath, and hot shivers went coursing over my body. I was paid my winnings in banknotes, amounting to a total of four thousand florins and eighty friedrichs (I was still able to calculate the amounts at that point).

After that, I remember, I again staked two thousand florins on the twelve middle numbers, and lost. Then I staked my gold, my eighty gold friedrichs, and lost. Then madness seemed to grip me, and seizing my last two thousand florins, I staked them on the twelve first numbers, totally at random and without any sort of calculation. When I had done so, there followed a moment of suspense comparable only to that which Madame Blanchard[48] must have experienced when she was falling to the ground from her balloon in Paris.

'Quatre!' called the croupier.

With the addition of my original stake, I was now in possession of six thousand florins! Once more I looked around me like a conqueror, once more I feared nothing as I threw down four thousand of these florins on black. Nine other people followed my example. The croupiers glanced at each other and exchanged a few words; the bystanders murmured expectantly.

The ball landed on black. After that I don't exactly remember the amounts or the order of my bets. I only remember that, as if in a dream, I won sixteen thousand florins in one round; that in the three following rounds, I lost twelve thousand; that I moved the remaining four thousand on to 'Passe' (though quite unconscious of what I was doing – I was merely playing, as it were, mechanically, without reflection, waiting for something) and won; and that I then won four more times in a row. I can remember raking in money in thousands, most frequently on the twelve middle numbers, which I stuck to, and which kept appearing in a sort of regular order – first, three or four times running, and then, after an interval of a couple of rounds, in another break of three or four appearances. Sometimes, this astonishing sort of regularity comes in patches, which upsets all the calculations of gamblers who play with a pencil and notebook in their hands. Fortune plays some terrible tricks at roulette!

Not more than half an hour could have passed since I had entered the casino. Suddenly a croupier informed me that I had won thirty thousand florins, and that, since that was the limit for which the bank could make itself responsible at any one time, roulette at that table must close for the night. Accordingly, I picked up my pile of gold, stuffed it into my pockets, and, grasping my sheaf of banknotes, moved to the table in an adjoining salon where a second game of roulette was in progress. The crowd followed me in a body, and cleared a place for me at the table; after which, I proceeded to stake as before – that is to say, randomly and without making calculations. What saved me from ruin I do not know.

Of course, there were times when some minor calculating *did* flash through my mind. For instance, I would keep to certain figures and combinations for a while, then abandon them again before long, without knowing what I was doing. In fact, I can't have been in possession of all my faculties, as I can remember the croupiers correcting my play more than once, owing to my having made some serious mistake. My brows were damp with sweat, and my hands were shaking. Some of these Poles gathered round me to offer their services, but I paid no attention to any of them. Nor did my luck fail me now. Suddenly, there arose around me a loud din of talking and laughter; there were shouts of 'Bravo, bravo!' and some people even clapped. I had raked in thirty thousand florins, and again the bank had had to close for the night!

'Leave now, leave now,' a voice whispered to me on my right. The person who had spoken to me was a Jew from Frankfurt, a man who had been standing beside me the whole time, occasionally helping me in my play.

'Yes, for God's sake, go,' whispered a second voice in my left ear. Glancing around, I saw a modestly and plainly dressed lady not thirty years old, a woman whose face, though pale and sickly-looking, bore clear traces of former beauty. At that moment, I was stuffing the crumpled banknotes into my pockets and collecting up all the gold that was left on the table. Seizing my last five hundred gulden note, I contrived to slip it unperceived into the hand of the pale lady. An overpowering impulse had made me do so, and I remember how her thin little fingers pressed mine in token of her deep gratitude. It was all done in a flash.

Having picked all my winnings, I walked over to where trente-et-quarante was being played, a game that boasts a more aristocratic public. It's played with cards instead of a wheel. Here the bank will pay up to a limit of a hundred thousand thalers, but the highest stake permitted is, as in roulette, four thousand florins. Although I knew nothing about the game – I scarcely knew what you could wager on, except that you could bet on black and red, as in roulette – I joined the circle of players, while the rest of the crowd gathered round me. At this distance of time I can't remember whether I ever gave a thought to Polina. I was only conscious of a vague pleasure in raking in and grabbing the banknotes which kept piling up in front of me.

But, as before, Fortune seemed to be backing me. As though planned, there came to my aid a circumstance which occurs not infrequently in gambling. The circumstance is that luck quite often attaches itself to, say, red, and does not leave it for, say, ten, or even fifteen, rounds in succession. Three days earlier, I had heard that, during the previous week there had been a run of twenty-two consecutive wins on red – an occurrence never before known at roulette, and talked of with astonishment. Naturally enough, what happens in such circumstances is that many desert red after ten or a dozen rounds, but nevertheless no experienced gambler will stake anything on black (the opposite of red) either, because every experienced player knows the meaning of 'capricious Fortune'. That is to say, after, say, the sixteenth win of red, one would think that in the seventeenth round the ball would inevitably come to rest on black, so novices are apt to back the latter in the seventeenth round. They even double or treble their stakes on it, only to lose heavily.

Yet some whim or other led me, on noticing that red had come up seven times in a row, to fix on that colour. Probably this was mostly due to conceit, because I wanted to astonish the bystanders with the riskiness of my play. Also, I remember that – and oh, what a strange sensation it was! – I suddenly, and even without being pushed to do so by my vanity, became driven by a *desire* to take risks. If one's spirit has passed through a great many sensations, possibly it can no longer be satisfied by them, but grows more aroused and demands more sensations, stronger and stronger ones, until at length it collapses exhausted. Certainly, if the rules of the game had allowed me to stake fifty thousand florins at a time, I would have done so. All around me, I could hear exclamations that the whole thing was crazy, since red had won fourteen times already!

'Monsieur a gagné déjà cent mille florins,'[49] a voice beside me exclaimed.

I came to my senses. What? I'd won a hundred thousand florins that evening? If so, what more did I need to win? I seized the banknotes, stuffed them into my pockets, collected together the gold without counting it, and started to leave the casino. As I passed through the salons, people smiled to see my bulging pockets and unsteady gait – the gold I was carrying must have weighed a good twenty pounds or so! I saw several hands stretched out towards me, and as I passed I filled them with all the money that I could grasp in my own. At length two Jews stopped me near the exit.

'You're a brave young man, very brave,' one said, 'but make sure you leave early tomorrow, as early as you can, because if you don't you'll lose everything you've won.'

But I didn't pay any attention to them. The avenue was so dark you could hardly see your hands in front of your face, and it was about half a mile to the hotel, but I wasn't afraid of robbers or pickpockets. I never have been since I was a boy. I can't remember what I thought about on the way back. All I felt was a sort of terrible pleasure, the pleasure of . . . (how can I best express it?) . . . of success, of conquest, of power. Before my eyes there flitted the image of Polina, and I kept remembering, and reminding myself, that it was *her* I was going to, that it was in *her* presence I would soon be standing, that it was *her* to whom I would soon be able to tell the whole story. I scarcely remembered what she had said to me not long before, or the reason why I had left her, or all those varied sensations which I had been experiencing barely an hour and a half before. No, those sensations seemed to be things of the past, things that had sorted themselves out and become obsolete, things about which we would need to trouble ourselves no longer, since, for us, life was about to begin anew. I had just reached the end of the avenue when the thought came to me, 'But what if I *was* robbed or murdered now?' With each step the fear increased until, in my terror, I almost started to run. Suddenly, as I came out of the avenue, there were the lights of the hotel, the twinkling of a myriad lamps! Yes, thanks be to God, I was home!

Running up to my room, I flung open the door. Polina was still on the sofa, with a lighted candle in front of her, and her hands clasped.

As I entered, she stared at me in astonishment – for, truth to tell, at that moment I must have been a strange sight. I stood in front of her, and started to throw my piles of money on to the table.

XV

I remember how she gazed intently into my face, without moving from her place or changing her position.

'I've won two hundred thousand francs!' I exclaimed as I pulled out my last roll of banknotes. The pile of money covered the whole table. I couldn't take my eyes off it. Consequently, for a moment or two I was no longer thinking about Polina. I began to put the money into some order, to fold the banknotes together and gather the gold into a separate pile. That done, I left everything where it was lying, and started to pace up and down the room with rapid strides, lost in thought. Then I darted over to the table once more, and began to re-count the money, until all of a sudden, as if I had just remembered something, I rushed to the door, closed it and double-locked it. Finally I stopped in front of my little suitcase, wondering what to do.

'Should I put the money in there until tomorrow?' I asked, turning round to Polina sharply as I remembered about her again.

She was still in the same place, still not making a sound. But her eyes were following my every movement. There was a strange expression on her face, an expression I didn't like. I don't think I would be wrong if I said it was a look of sheer hatred.

I quickly walked over to her.

'Polina,' I said, 'here are twenty-five thousand florins, that's fifty thousand francs or more. Take them, and tomorrow go and throw them in De Griers' face.'

She didn't answer.

'Or, if you prefer,' I continued, 'let me take them to him myself tomorrow, yes, early tomorrow morning. Shall I do that?'

Then all at once she burst out laughing, and went on laughing for a long while. I looked at her in astonishment, feeling rather offended. Her laughter was too like the derisive laughter she had so often indulged in of late, laughter that had always erupted when I was in the middle of my most ardent confessions. Eventually she stopped, and frowned at me.

'I'm not going to take your money,' she said contemptuously.

'Why not?' I shouted. 'Why ever not, Polina?'

'Because I'm not in the habit of taking money for nothing.'

'But I'm offering it to you as a friend, just as I offer you my very life.'

At this she gave me a long, penetrating look, as if she was trying to pierce me with it.

'You're paying too much for me,' she remarked with a smile. 'De Griers' mistress isn't worth fifty thousand francs.'

'Oh Polina, how can you talk like that?' I exclaimed reproachfully. 'Am I De Griers?'

'You?' she cried, with her eyes suddenly flashing. 'I *hate* you! Yes, I do, I *hate* you! I don't love you any more than I do De Griers.'

Then she buried her face in her hands and collapsed into hysterics. I rushed to her side. I somehow had an inkling that something had happened to her which had nothing to do with me. She was like someone who had gone temporarily insane.

'Buy me, would you? Is that what you want to do? Buy me for fifty thousand francs like De Griers is trying to do?' she gasped out, between convulsive sobs.

I held her in my arms, kissed her hands and feet, and went down on my knees in front of her.

Presently the fit of hysterics subsided, and, laying her hands on my shoulders, she gazed for a while into my face, as though trying to read it. She was listening to what I said to her, but it was obvious she wasn't really taking it in. Her face looked so dark and despondent that I began to fear for her sanity. One moment she would be pulling me towards her, a trustful smile playing over her face; and then, just as suddenly, she would push me away again, glowering at me.

Finally she threw herself at me to embrace me.

'You love me, don't you?' she said. 'You do, don't you, since you were even willing to quarrel with the Baron when I asked you to?'

Then she laughed, laughing as if she had just remembered something amusing and rather endearing. She was laughing and crying at the

same time. What was I to do? I was like a man with a fever. I remember
she began to say something to me, though I had no idea what she was
saying, because she was speaking in a sort of delirium, babbling as if
she was trying to tell me something very quickly. Now and then she
would break into that smile I was beginning to dread. 'No, no!' she
kept repeating. '*You* are my loved one, *you* are the man I trust.' Again
she put her hands on my shoulders, and again she gazed at me as she
repeated: '*You* love me. You *do* love me. Will you *always* love me?' I
couldn't take my eyes off her. Never before had I seen her in this mood
of tenderness and affection. True, the mood was the result of hysteria,
but what of that? All of a sudden, noticing my ardent looks, she smiled
slightly and for no apparent reason began to talk about Astley.

She went on and on talking about him, but I couldn't make out all
she said, more particularly when she was endeavouring to tell me about
something or other which had happened recently. On the whole, she
appeared to be laughing at Astley, as she kept repeating that he was
waiting for her, and didn't I know that, even at that moment, he was
probably standing beneath the window? 'Yes, yes, he's there, he's
there,' she said. 'Open the window and see if he isn't.' She was pushing
me in the direction of the window, but no sooner did I make a movement towards it than she burst out laughing, and I stayed beside her
and she embraced me.

'Shall we go away, then? Shall we leave tomorrow?' she asked as
the thought came into her troubled mind. 'How would it be if we tried
to catch up with Grandmother? I think we might catch up with her in
Berlin. And what do you think she would say when we did catch with
her and she first caught sight of us? And what about Mr Astley? *He*
wouldn't jump from the Schlangenberg for my sake! No! I'm quite
sure about that!' – and she laughed. 'Do you know where he's going
next year? He says he intends to go to the North Pole for scientific
study, and has invited me to go with him! Ha, ha, ha! He also says
that we Russians know nothing, and can do nothing without European
help. But he's a good fellow all the same. For instance, he doesn't
blame the General over all this, but says that Mademoiselle Blanche . . .

that love . . . oh, but I don't know, I don't know.' She stopped suddenly, as though she had said all she wanted to say, or else had lost the thread and was confused. 'The poor things, I'm really sorry for them, and for Grandmother . . . But how could you think you could kill De Griers? Did you really, really think you could kill him? You fool! Do you suppose I would *allow* you to fight De Griers? And you won't be killing the Baron either.' Here she burst out laughing again. 'How absurd you looked when you were talking to the Burmerhelms! I was watching you all the time, watching you from where I was sitting. And how unwilling you were to go when I sent you! Oh, how I laughed and laughed!' And she gave another laugh.

Then she kissed and embraced me again, once again pressing her face to mine with tender passion. I neither saw nor heard her, my head was in such a whirl.

It must have been about seven o'clock in the morning when I awoke. Light was shining into the room, and Polina was sitting by my side with a strange expression on her face, as though she had seen some dark vision and was unable to collect her thoughts. She, too, had just woken up and was staring at the money on the table. My head ached; it felt heavy. I tried to take Polina's hand, but she pushed me away and jumped up from the sofa. It was a grey dawn and it had been raining, but nevertheless she walked over to the window, opened it, and, leaning on the window-sill, stuck her head out to get some air. She remained like that for several minutes, without looking round at me or listening to what I was saying. Into my head there came the uneasy thought: What's going to happen now? How is all this going to end? Suddenly Polina rose from the window, walked over the table, and, looking at me with an expression of deep hatred, her lips quivering with anger, said:

'Right, give me my fifty thousand francs!'

'Polina, you say that now? Again now?' I exclaimed.

'So you've changed your mind, then? Ha, ha, ha! Are you sorry you ever promised me them?'

On the table where, the previous night, I had counted out the money, there was still a packet of twenty-five thousand florins. I handed it to her.

'The francs are mine, then, are they? They're mine?' she asked spitefully, holding the money in her hands.

'Yes, they've always been yours,' I said.

'Then *take* your fifty thousand francs!' she said, and hurled them right in my face. The packet burst as she did so, and the floor was covered with banknotes. The instant the deed was done, she rushed out of the room.

At that moment she can't have been in her right mind, but what the cause of her temporary fit of madness was I cannot say. For the past month she had been unwell. But what had brought about her *present* state of mind, and above all things, this sudden outburst? Was it due to wounded pride? Was it despair over her decision to come to me? Was it that, making too much of my good fortune, I had seemed to be intending to desert her (just as De Griers had done) once I'd given her the fifty thousand francs? But, on my honour, I had never had any such intention. What was at fault, I think – even though she didn't realise it herself – was her own pride, which kept driving her not to trust me but instead to insult me. In her eyes I was just like De Griers, and therefore had been condemned for a fault that was not my own. Her mood of late had been a sort of madness, she was almost deranged. I knew that perfectly well, but I had never taken it sufficiently into consideration. Perhaps that was what she couldn't forgive. Yes, but if that accounts for now, what about earlier? Her delirium and sickness were not so bad as to make her unaware of what she was doing when she brought me De Griers' letter. No, she must have known what she was doing then.

Somehow I managed to stuff the pile of notes and gold under the bed and conceal them, and left the room some ten minutes after Polina. I felt sure she had gone back to her own room, so I decided to follow her quietly and ask the nanny, when she opened the door, how her mistress was. Imagine my surprise, therefore, when I met the nanny on the stairs and she informed me that Polina had not yet returned, and that she (the nanny) was at that very moment on her way to my room to find her!

'Mademoiselle left me only ten minutes ago,' I said. 'What can have become of her?'

The nanny looked at me reproachfully.

There were already rumours flying round the hotel. Both in the porter's lodge and in the head waiter's office it was being whispered that, at seven o'clock that morning, the young lady had left the hotel and rushed off, in the rain, in the direction of the Hôtel d'Angleterre. From what was said and what was hinted at, I could tell that the fact that Polina had spent the night in my room was now public knowledge. Moreover, there were rumours circulating about the General's family affairs. It was known that last night he had gone mad and wandered round the hotel in tears; also that the old lady who had arrived was his mother, and that she had come from Russia with the express purpose of forbidding her son's marriage with Mademoiselle de Cominges, and to cut him out of her will if he disobeyed her; and that, because he *had* disobeyed her, she had deliberately squandered all her money at roulette in order to have nothing to leave to him. 'Oh, these Russians!' exclaimed the head waiter, shaking his head indignantly. The people standing nearby laughed. The head waiter was preparing my bill. Everyone knew about my winnings; Karl, the corridor footman, was the first to congratulate me. But I had no time to spend with these people. I needed to make for the Hôtel d'Angleterre as fast as I could.

It was very early in the day for Mr Astley to receive visitors, but as soon as he learnt that it was me who had arrived, he came out into the corridor to meet me and stood looking at me in silence with his steel-grey eyes as he waited to hear what I had to say. I inquired after Polina.

'She's ill,' he replied, still looking at me with his direct, unwavering glance.

'And she's in your rooms.'

'Yes, she's in my rooms.'

'And you intend to keep her there?'

'Yes, I intend to keep her there.'

'But, Mr Astley, that will cause a scandal. It ought not to be allowed. Besides, she's very ill. Perhaps you hadn't noticed that?'

'Yes, I have. It was me who told you about it. If she hadn't been ill, she wouldn't have gone to your room and spent the night with you.'

'So you know all about that?'

'Yes, because last night she was to have gone with me to the house of a relative of mine. Unfortunately, being unwell, she made a mistake and went to your rooms instead.'

'Indeed? Then I wish you every happiness, Mr Astley. By the way, you've reminded me of something. Were you beneath my window last night? Over and over again Miss Polina kept telling me to open the window and see if you were there, after which she always smiled.'

'Indeed? No, I wasn't there; but I was waiting in the corridor, and walking around the hotel.'

'She should see a doctor, you know, Mr Astley.'

'Yes, she should. I've sent for one, and, if she dies, I shall hold you responsible.'

This astounded me.

'I beg your pardon, Mr Astley,' I replied, 'but what is it you want?'

'Tell me, is it true that you won two hundred thousand thalers last night?'

'No, I only won a hundred thousand florins.'

'Good heavens! Then I suppose you'll be off to Paris this morning?'

'Why?'

'All Russians who have money go to Paris,' explained Astley, in a tone of voice that sounded as if he was reading it out of a book.

'But what could I do in Paris now, in the summertime? I love her, Mr Astley! Surely you know that?'

'Really? I'm quite sure you *don't*. In any case, if you were to stay here, you would lose everything you have, and have nothing left to pay your trip to Paris with. Well, goodbye now. I feel sure that today will see you gone from here.'

'Goodbye, then. But I'm *not* going to Paris. Just think for a moment,

Mr Astley, what is to become of this family? I mean, there's the General . . . and this business with Miss Polina will soon be all over town.'

'I daresay, but I hardly think that will break the General's heart; he has other things on his mind. Besides, Miss Polina has a perfect right to live where she chooses. In short, one could say that this family, as a family, has ceased to exist.'

I walked away, smiling to myself at the Englishman's strange certainty that I would soon be leaving for Paris. 'I suppose he'll want to shoot me in a duel if Polina dies, and what a business that would be.' Now, although I was honestly sorry for Polina, it's a fact that from the moment when, the previous night, I had approached the gaming-tables and had begun to rake in the piles of money, my love for her had become less important to me. Yes, I can say that now, although at the time I was barely conscious of it. Am I, then, basically a gambler? Had I really loved Polina so . . . so strangely? No, no! As God is my witness, I *do* love her, I love her still! Even when I was returning home from Mr Astley's my suffering was genuine, and my self-reproach sincere. But I was soon to go through an exceedingly strange and unpleasant experience.

I was heading for the General's rooms when I heard a door open close to me and a voice call me by name. It was Mademoiselle Blanche's mother, the Widow de Cominges, who was inviting me, on behalf of her daughter, to come in.

It wasn't a big suite, just two rooms. When I went in, I heard someone laughing and shouting from the bedroom, where Mademoiselle Blanche was just getting up.

'Oh, c'est lui!! Viens donc, bêtà! Is it true que tu as gagné une montagne d'or et d'argent? J'aimerais mieux l'or.'[50]

'Yes,' I replied with a smile.

'How much?'

'A hundred thousand florins.'

'Bibi, comme tu es bête! Come in here, because I can't hear you where you are now. Nous ferons bombance, n'est-ce pas?'[51]

Entering her room, I found her lolling under a pink satin bedspread, revealing a pair of swarthy, strong, stunning shoulders – shoulders such as one only sees in dreams – covered by a white cambric nightgown trimmed with lace, which stood out in striking contrast against the darkness of her skin.

'Mon fils, as-tu du coeur?'[52] she exclaimed when she saw me, and then giggled. Her laugh had always been cheerful. At times it was even sincere.

'Tout autre . . .' I began, paraphrasing Corneille[53].

'First of all,' she prattled on, 'look for my stockings and help me get my shoes on. And then, si tu n'es pas trop bête, je te prends à Paris.[54] I'm leaving right away, you know.'

'Right now?'

'In half an hour.'

Sure enough, all her trunks and suitcases were standing there already packed. Coffee had been served much earlier.

'Eh bien, if you like, tu verras Paris. Dis donc, qu'est-ce que c'est qu'un "outchitel"? Tu étais bien bête quand tu étais "outchitel".[55] Where are my stockings? Help me put them on.'

And she lifted up a really ravishing foot – small, dark-skinned, and not misshapen like the majority of feet which look dainty only in shoes. I laughed, and started to pull a silk stocking on to her foot, while Mademoiselle Blanche sat on the edge of the bed, chattering away.

'Eh bien, que feras-tu si je te prends avec moi? First of all, I want fifty thousand francs, and you shall give them to me in Frankfurt. Then we'll go on to Paris, where we will live together, et je te ferai voir des étoiles en plein jour.[56] Yes, you'll see women like you've never seen before.'

'Stop a moment. If I were to give you those fifty thousand francs, what would I have left for myself?'

'The other hundred and fifty thousand francs, remember. Besides, I'm prepared to live with you in your rooms for a month, or two months, or whatever. But it wouldn't take us more than two months to get through that hundred and fifty thousand, because je suis bonne enfant and I like a good time – I'm telling you that now – mais tu verras des étoiles.'[57]

'What? You mean to say we would spend the whole lot in two months?'

'Certainly. Does that surprise you very much? Ah, vil esclave![58] Why, one month of that life would be better than the whole of your previous existence. One month – et après, le déluge![59] Mais tu ne peux comprendre, va! Away with you! You're not worth it. Hey, que fais-tu?'[60]

The reason for this last exclamation was that, while pulling on the other stocking, I felt I just had to kiss her. Immediately she drew back, kicked me in the face with her toes, and chased me out of the room.

'Eh bien, mon "outchitel",' she called after me, 'je t'attends, si tu veux.[61] I'm setting off in a quarter of an hour's time.'

I returned to my own room with my head in a whirl. It was not my fault that Polina had thrown the money in my face and preferred Mr Astley to myself. A few banknotes were still scattered about the floor and I picked them up. At that moment the door opened, and the head waiter appeared, a person who, until now, had never bestowed upon me so much as a glance. He had come to know if I would prefer to move to a lower floor, to a magnificent suite which Count V. had just left.

I thought about it for a moment.

'No!' I shouted. 'Get me my bill, please, I'll be leaving in ten minutes.'

'To Paris, then, if to Paris it's to be!' I added to myself. 'It's been my destiny since the day I was born.'

Within a quarter of an hour all three of us were seated in a family compartment – Mademoiselle Blanche, the Widow de Cominges and myself. Blanche was laughing almost hysterically as she looked at me, and so was her mother, but I wasn't feeling so cheerful. My life had been broken in two, but since yesterday I had grown used to staking everything on the turn of a card. Perhaps it was the case that all this sudden wealth was too much for me and that I had taken leave of my senses. But perhaps I couldn't have asked for anything more. There was going to be a change of scene, but I thought it would only be for a short while. 'Within a month from now,' I kept thinking to myself, 'I'll be back in Roulettenburg again, and *then* I mean to have it out with you, Mr Astley!' As I look back at things now, I remember that I felt very depressed, though I managed to laugh back at that foolish girl Blanche.

'What's the matter with you? How silly you are! How silly you are!' she exclaimed at length, breaking off from her laughter to seriously reproach me. 'Come on! We're going to spend your two hundred thousand francs for you, et tu seras heureux comme un petit roi.[62] I'll tie your cravat for you, and introduce you to Hortense. And when we've spent your money you'll come back here and break the bank again. What did those two Jews tell you? That what you need most is courage, and that you've got it. So this is not the only time you'll be hurrying to Paris with money in your pocket. Quant à moi, je veux cinquante mille francs de rente, et alors—'[63]

'But what about the General?' I interrupted.

'The General? You know well enough that at about this time every day he goes to buy me a bouquet. On this occasion, I took care to tell him that he had to search for the choicest flowers, and when he returns home, the poor fellow will find the bird flown. He'll take wing in pursuit, you'll see. Ha, ha, ha! And I won't be sorry if he does, because he could be useful to me in Paris, and Mr Astley will pay his debts here.'

This was how I left for Paris.

XVI

What can I say about Paris? The whole affair was crazy, sheer madness. I spent a little over three weeks there and in that time saw my hundred thousand francs disappear. I say my hundred thousand francs because I gave the other hundred thousand to Mademoiselle Blanche in cash. I gave her fifty thousand francs in Frankfurt and, three days later, in Paris, advanced her another fifty thousand in the form of a promissory note. Nevertheless, a week had not gone by before she came to me for that money too. 'Et les cent mille francs qui nous restent,' she added, 'tu les mangeras avec moi, mon outchitel.'[64] Yes, she always called me her 'outchitel', her 'tutor'. Anyone more scrimping, grasping and stingy than Mademoiselle Blanche one could not imagine, but only with respect to *her own* money. She needed *my* hundred thousand (as she explained to me later) to get herself set up in Paris, 'so that once and for all I may live in a respectable style, protected for a long time to come against any stones that Fortune may fling at me.' Nevertheless, I didn't see anything of those hundred thousand francs, because my own purse (which she inspected daily) never managed to have more than a hundred francs in it at a time, and usually not even that much.

'What do you want with money?' she would say to me with an air of total simplicity, and I never argued the point. She fitted out her flat very nicely with the money, which did not stop her saying when, later, she was showing me over the rooms of her new home: 'See what care and taste can do with the most scanty means.' That 'scantiness', however, had cost me fifty thousand francs! With the remaining fifty thousand she purchased a carriage and horses. Also, we gave a couple of balls, evening parties attended by Hortense and Lisette and Cléopâtre, women remarkable both for the number of their liaisons and (though only in some cases) for their good looks. At these gatherings I had to play the ridiculous role of host, to meet and entertain fat parvenu merchants, unbearable both in their rudeness and their boasting, colonels of various kinds, starving authors and journalistic hacks – all in fashionable tailcoats and pale yellow gloves and displaying such conceit and boastfulness as would be unthinkable even in St Petersburg – and that's saying a lot! They used to make fun of me, but I would console myself by drinking champagne and retreating to a side-room. Nevertheless, I found the whole thing loathsome. 'C'est un outchitel,' Blanche would say of me, 'qui a gagné deux cent mille francs[65], and but for me, would have had no idea how to spend it all. Soon he'll have to return to his tutoring. Does anyone know of a vacant post? One must do something for him, you know.'

I frequently had recourse to champagne because I constantly felt depressed and bored, owing to the fact that I was living in the most bourgeois, mercenary milieu imaginable, where every sou was counted and grudged. Indeed, two weeks had not gone by before I realised that Blanche had no real affection for me, even though she dressed me in elegant clothes, and tied my cravat herself every day. Quite simply, she utterly despised me. But that didn't bother me at all. Bored and depressed, I generally spent my evenings at the Château des Fleurs, where I would get drunk and dance the cancan (which, in that establishment, was performed pretty indecently) with some distinction. At length, the time came when Blanche had drained my purse dry. She had conceived an idea that, during the time of our residence together, it would be a good thing if I were always to walk behind her with a paper and pencil, in order to jot down exactly what she spent and what she stole, and what she was going to spend and going to steal. Well, of course I couldn't fail to be aware that this would entail a battle over every ten-franc piece, so although she had prepared a suitable answer to every possible objection I might make, she soon saw that I made no objections at all and therefore had to start the arguments herself. She would burst out into tirades which were met only with silence as I lolled on a sofa and stared fixedly at the ceiling. This greatly surprised her. At first she imagined that it was due merely to the fact that I was a fool, 'un outchitel', so she would break off her harangue in the belief that, being too stupid to understand, I was a hopeless case. Then she would leave the room, but return ten minutes later to resume the battle.

This continued throughout the time she was squandering my money, frittering it away well out of proportion to our means; one example was the way she changed her first pair of horses for a pair that cost sixteen thousand francs.

'My pet,' she said on the latter occasion as she came over to me, 'surely you're not angry with me?'

'No, you just make me weary,' was my reply, as I pushed her away from me. This seemed so odd to her that she immediately sat down beside me.

'You see,' she went on, 'I only decided to spend that much on these horses because I can easily sell them again. They would go at any time for *twenty* thousand francs.'

'Yes, yes. They're splendid horses, you've got a splendid carriage and pair. I am perfectly content. Say nothing more about it.'

'Then you're not angry?'

'No. Why should I be? You're wise to provide yourself with what you need, because it will all come in handy in the future. Yes, I quite see the necessity of your establishing yourself on a solid basis, because without that you'll never make a million. My hundred thousand francs I look on as merely a beginning, a mere drop in the ocean.'

Blanche, who had by no means been expecting such declarations from me but rather an argument and protests, was rather taken aback.

'Well, so that's the sort of man you are!' she exclaimed. 'Mais tu as l'esprit pour comprendre. Sais-tu, mon garçon[66], although you're a tutor, you ought to have been born a prince. Aren't you sorry that your money is disappearing so quickly?'

'No. The quicker it goes, the better.'

'Mais – sais-tu – mais dis donc, you're not really rich, are you? Mais sais-tu, you have too much contempt for money. Qu'est-ce que tu feras après, dis donc?'[67]

'"Après", I shall go to Homburg and win another hundred thousand francs.'

'Oui, oui, c'est ça, c'est magnifique! Oh, I know you'll win the money, and then you'll bring it here to me. Dis donc, you'll succeed in making me love you. Since you are what you are, I mean to love you all the time and never be unfaithful to you. You see, I haven't loved you up till now parce que je croyais que tu n'es qu'un outchitel (quelque chose comme un laquais, n'est-ce pas?), yet I've been true to you all this time, parce que je suis bonne fille.'[68]

'You're lying!' I broke in. 'Didn't I see you the other day with Albert, that swarthy little officer?'

'Oh, oh! Mais tu es—'

'Yes, you're lying all right. But what makes you think that I'd be angry? Rubbish! Il faut que jeunesse se passe.[69] Even if that officer was here now, I wouldn't throw him out of the room if I thought you really cared for him. But just don't give him any of my money, do you hear?'

'So you're saying you wouldn't be angry? Mais tu es un vrai philosophe, sais-tu? Oui, un vrai philosophe! Eh bien, je t'aimerai, je t'aimerai. Tu verras, tu seras content.'[70]

True enough, from that time on she seemed to attach herself only to me, and in this manner we spent our last ten days together. The promised 'étoiles' I never did see, but in other respects she, to a certain extent, kept her word. Moreover, she introduced me to Hortense, who was a remarkable woman in her way, and known among us as Thérèse the philosopher.

But there's no need to enlarge on all that, because to do so would require a whole story to itself, with a flavour of its own which I am loth to impart to the present tale. The point is that with all my heart and soul I wanted the episode to come to an end as quickly as possible. Unfortunately, our hundred thousand francs lasted us, as I have said, for very nearly a month, which really surprised me. At all events, Blanche bought things for herself to the tune of eighty thousand francs, and the rest just sufficed to meet our living expenses. Towards the end of the affair, Blanche became almost frank with me (at least, didn't lie to me about *some* things), declaring, for example, that none of the debts she had been obliged to incur were going to fall on my head. 'I have deliberately refrained from making you responsible for any of

my bills or what I have borrowed,' she said, 'because I'm sorry for
you. Any other woman in my place would have done so, and let you
go to prison. See, then, how much I love you, and how kind-hearted
I am! Just think what this blessed marriage to the General is going to
cost me!'

Sure enough, there was a wedding. It took place at the end of our
month together, and I am bound to suppose that it was on that ceremony
that the last remnants of my money were spent. With it our time
together came to an end, and I formally retired from the scene.

This is how it happened: A week after we had taken up residence
in Paris, the General arrived there. He came straight to see us, and
from then on lived with us practically as our guest, though he had a
flat of his own as well. Blanche greeted him with laughter and shrieks
of delight, and even threw her arms around him. In fact, from then on
she made him follow her everywhere, whether walking along the
boulevards, or when out driving, or when going to the theatre, or when
visiting people. The General was well suited to this. Still imposing in
appearance, and quite tall, he had a dyed moustache and whiskers (he
had formerly been in the cuirassiers) and a handsome, if somewhat
wrinkled, face. What's more, his manners were impeccable, and he
wore a frockcoat well, the more so since, in Paris, he took to wearing
his medals. To promenade along the boulevards with such a man was
not only possible but, so to speak, to be recommended, and with this
plan the kind but foolish General found nothing at all to object to. The
truth is, he had never been expecting all this when he came to Paris
to seek us out. When he had made his first appearance, he was virtually quaking with terror, because he'd been expecting Blanche to
immediately create a fuss and have him turned away from the door,
for which reason he was all the more delighted at the turn things had
taken and spent the month in a state of mindless ecstasy. I later learnt
that, after our unexpected departure from Roulettenburg, he had had
a sort of a fit and fallen unconscious, after which he'd spent a week
in a sort of rambling delirium. Doctors had been summoned to him,
but he had suddenly dismissed them and taken a train to Paris. Of

course Blanche's reception of him had acted as the best of all possible cures, but for long enough he carried the marks of his affliction despite his present state of rapture and delight. To think clearly, or even to engage in any serious conversation, had now become impossible for him; he could only answer 'Hm!' to whatever was said to him and then nod his head in confirmation. Sometimes he would laugh, but in a nervous, hysterical way, while at other times he would sit for hours looking as black as night, with his heavy eyebrows knitted in a frown. Of much that was going on he remained completely unaware, because he had become extremely absent-minded and had taken to talking to himself. Only Blanche could awake in him any semblance of life. His fits of depression and moodiness, sitting in corners, always meant either that he had not seen her for some time, or that she had gone out without taking him with her, or that she had omitted to embrace him before leaving. When in this condition, he was unable to say what he wanted, nor had he the slightest idea that he was sulking and moping like this. After being in this condition for an hour or two (this I noticed on two occasions when Blanche had gone out for the day – probably to see Albert), he would begin to look around him, and grow uneasy, and rush about as if he'd suddenly remembered something and had to find it; then, not finding the object of his search, nor even remembering what it was he thought he'd been looking for, he would just as suddenly relapse into oblivion, and continue in that state until Blanche reappeared – cheerful, playful, dressed up to the nines, and laughing her strident laugh as she went over to tease him, or even kiss him (though this latter reward he seldom received). Once, he was so overjoyed to see her that he burst into tears. I was quite astonished.

From the moment of his arrival in Paris, Blanche began to plead with me on his behalf, and at such times she rose to heights of eloquence, saying that it was for *me* she had abandoned him, though she had almost become his betrothed and had promised that she would be; that it was for *her* sake he had deserted his family; that I had been in his service and ought to remember that and feel ashamed. To all this I would say nothing, however much she prattled on, until at length I would burst out laughing and the incident would come to an end (at first, as I have said, she thought me a fool, but then came to look on me as a man of sense and sensibility). In short, I had the pleasure of calling her better nature into play, for although at first I had not thought her so, she was in reality a kind-hearted woman – after her own fashion. 'You're good and clever,' she said to me at the end, 'and my one regret is that you're so foolish. You'll never, ever be rich!'

'Un vrai russe, un calmouk,'[71] she usually called me.

Several times she sent me out to take the General for an airing in the streets, just as she might have done with a servant and a pet spaniel, but I preferred to take him to the theatre, to the Bal Mabille[72] and to restaurants. For this purpose she usually allowed me some money, though the General had a little of his own and enjoyed taking out his purse in front of other people. Once I actually had to forcibly prevent him from spending seven hundred francs on a brooch that had caught his eye in the Palais Royal[73] and that he wanted to buy as a present for Blanche. What was a seven-hundred-franc brooch to her? And all the General had in the world was a thousand francs! The source of even that money I could never determine, but I imagined it to have come from Mr Astley, the more particularly since it was he who had settled the family's hotel bill.

As to what the General thought of me, I think he never guessed my relationship with Blanche. True, he had heard, in a vague sort of way, that I had won a good deal of money, but he probably supposed me to be acting as secretary, or even as a kind of servant, to his beloved. At all events, he continued to address me in his old haughty style, as my superior. At times he even took it upon himself to scold me. One morning in particular, he started to sneer at me over our morning coffee. Though not a man prone to take offence, he suddenly, and for some reason I still don't understand, fell out with me. Of course he himself didn't even know the reason. Briefly, he began a speech which had neither beginning nor end, and cried out, à bâtons rompus[74], that I was just a boy, that he would teach me a lesson, that he would make me understand . . . and so on, and so on. No one could understand what he was saying, and eventually Blanche burst out laughing. Finally something calmed him down, and he was taken out for his walk. More than once, however, I noticed that his depression was getting worse, that he seemed to be feeling the lack of somebody or something, that, despite Blanche's presence, he was missing some person in particular. Twice, on these occasions, he plunged into a conversation with me, though he couldn't make himself intelligible and just went on rambling about his years in service, his late wife, his home and his property. Every now and then, also, some particular word would please him, and he would repeat it a hundred times in the day, even though the word expressed neither his thoughts nor his feelings. I would try to get him to talk about his children, but he always cut me short and moved on to another subject. 'Yes, yes, my children,' was all I could get out of him. 'Yes, you're right in what you have said about them.' Only once did he disclose his real feelings. That was when we were taking him to the theatre, and suddenly he exclaimed: 'Those unfortunate children! Oh, those unf – fo – fortunate children.' Once, too, when I chanced to mention Polina, he grew quite bitter against her. 'She's an ungrateful woman!' he exclaimed. 'She's a wicked and ungrateful woman! She's shamed the family. If there were laws here, I would have her brought to heel. Yes, I would.' As for De Griers, the General would not allow his name to be mentioned. 'He's ruined me,' he would say. 'He's robbed me and cut my throat. For two years he was a perfect nightmare to me. For months at a time he never left my dreams. Do not speak of him again.'

It was now clear to me that Blanche and he were on the point of coming to an arrangement, but, true to my usual habit, I said nothing. At length, Blanche took the initiative in explaining matters to me. This she did a week before we parted. 'Il a de la chance,'[75] she said, 'Grandmother is now *really* ill, and therefore bound to die. Mr Astley has just sent a telegram to say so, and you will no doubt agree with me that the General is likely to be her heir. Even if he isn't, he'll be all right, since, in the first place, he has his pension and, in the second place, he'll be content to live in a back room, and I shall be Madame

General and get into a good circle of society' (she was always thinking about this) 'and become a Russian landowner. Yes, I'll have a mansion of my own, and peasants, and I'll have my million.'

'But, what if he should get jealous? He might demand all sorts of things, you know. Do you follow me?'

'Oh, dear no! He wouldn't dare! Besides, I've taken steps to prevent that, don't you worry. That is to say, I've persuaded him to sign notes of hand in Albert's name. Consequently, I could get him punished at any time. So he won't dare.'

'Very well, then. Marry him.'

And, in fact, she did, though the marriage was a family one only, with no pomp or ceremony. She actually invited no one to the ceremony except Albert and a few other friends. Hortense, Cléopâtre and the rest she kept firmly at a distance. As for the bridegroom, he took a great interest in his new position. Blanche herself tied his cravat, and pomaded him, with the result that, dressed in his frockcoat and a white waistcoat, he looked très comme il faut[76].

'Il est pourtant très comme il faut,'[77] Blanche remarked when she came out of his room, as if the idea that he was 'très comme il faut' had surprised even her. I paid so little attention to what was going on, looking on merely as an idle spectator, that I have forgotten most of what happened. I only remember that Blanche and the Widow figured in it, not as 'De Cominges', but as 'Du Placet'. Why they had been 'De Cominges' up till then, I don't know; I only know that the General was entirely satisfied, that he liked the name 'Du Placet' even better than he had liked the name 'De Cominges'. On the morning of the wedding, he paced up and down the room in his wedding attire, repeating to himself with an air of great gravity and importance: 'Mademoiselle Blanche du Placet! Blanche du Placet! Du Placet! Miss Blanca dyu-Plaset!' He beamed with satisfaction as he did so. In the church, at the mayor's and at the wedding breakfast he was not only pleased and satisfied, but even proud. Blanche too underwent a change, now assuming an air of particular dignity.

'I must behave altogether differently,' she confided to me, looking serious. 'But there's one really annoying thing I had never thought of before, which is how best to pronounce my new family name. Zagoryansky, Zagoziansky, Madame la Générale de Zago-Zago – oh, these infernal Russian names. How about Madame la Générale de Fourteen Consonants! That last one would be the best to use, don't you think?'

At length the time had come for us to part, and Blanche, that silly Blanche, shed real tears as she took her leave of me. 'Tu étais bon enfant,' she said with a sob. 'Je te croyais bête et tu en avais l'air[78], but it suited you.' Then, having given me a final handshake, she exclaimed, 'Wait!', whereupon, running into her boudoir, she brought me out two thousand-franc notes. I could scarcely believe my eyes! 'They may come in handy for you,' she explained, 'for, though you're a very learned tutor, you're a very stupid man. More than two thousand francs, however, I'm not going to give you, because if I did, you would gamble it all away. Well, goodbye. Nous serons toujours bons amis, and if you win again, do not fail to come to me, et tu seras heureux.'[79]

I myself had still five hundred francs left, as well as a watch worth a thousand francs, a few diamond studs, and so on. Consequently, I could subsist for quite a length of time without worrying about it. I have deliberately settled in this little town partly to pull myself together and partly to wait for Mr Astley, who, I have learnt, will soon be here for a day or so on business. Yes, I'll find out all about everything, and then – then I shall go to Homburg. But I won't go to Roulettenburg until next year, because they say it's bad luck to try one's fortune twice in succession at the same table. Anyway, Homburg is where the best gambling is to be had.

XVII

It's a year and eight months since I last looked at these notes of mine. I do so now only because, being overwhelmed with depression, I wish to distract my mind by reading through them at random. I left off at the point where I was just going to Homburg. My God, with what a light heart (comparatively speaking) did I write those concluding lines! Well, perhaps not so much with a light heart as with a degree of self-confidence and unquenchable hope. At that time did I have any doubts about myself? Yet look at me now. Scarcely a year and a half have passed, but I'm worse off than the poorest beggar. But what is a beggar, anyhow? Who cares about being a beggar? I've just ruined myself, that's all. There's nothing I could compare my situation to at the moment, and moralising would serve no purpose in any case. At the present time nothing would be more absurd than moralising. And as for those self-satisfied people who, in their unctuous pride, are always ready to mouth their maxims, if only they knew how fully I myself understand the sordidness of my present state they wouldn't trouble to wag their tongues at me! What can they say to me that I don't already know? And is that the point in any case? The real point is this – that in a single turn of a roulette wheel, everything changes. Yet, had things turned out otherwise, these moralists would have been among the first (yes, I'm sure of it) to come up to me with congratulations and friendly banter. Yes, they would never have turned away from me as they do now! To hell with all of them! What am I now? Zero. Nothing. What will I be tomorrow? I may be resurrected from the dead and have begun life anew. Because I may still find the man in me, if my manhood has not yet been utterly destroyed.

As I say, I went to Homburg, but afterwards I went on to Roulettenburg and to Spa, as well as to Baden where I acted for a time as valet to a certain rascal of a Privy Councillor by the name of Heintze, who until lately was also my master here. Yes, for five months I lived my life with the servants! That was just after I had been released from

Roulettenburg prison, where I had spent some time for a small debt I owed. My release from prison was paid for by – well, by whom? By Mr Astley? By Polina? I don't know. At any rate, the debt was paid to the tune of two hundred thalers, and I sallied forth a free man. But what was I to do with myself? I ended up with this Heintze, who was a frivolous young man and idle with it, whereas I can speak and write in three languages. At first I acted as his secretary, at a salary of thirty gulden a month, but afterwards I became his footman, because he couldn't afford to keep a secretary and lowered my wages. I had nothing else to turn to, so I remained with him, and allowed myself to become his flunkey. But by stinting myself in food and drink I saved, during my five months of service, some seventy gulden, and one evening, when we were in Baden, I told him that I wished to resign my post and then rushed off to play roulette.

Oh, how my heart beat as I did so! No, it wasn't the money that I cared about. What I wanted was to make all this crowd of Heintzes, head waiters and fine ladies in Baden talk about me, recount my story, marvel at me, extol my successes and worship my winnings. True, these were childish fancies and aspirations, but, who knows? It was possible I might meet Polina and be able to tell her everything and see her look of surprise at how I had overcome so many adverse strokes of fortune. No, I had no desire for money for its own sake, because I was perfectly well aware that I would only squander it on some new Blanche and spend another three weeks in Paris driving a sixteen-thousand-franc pair of horses. I know I'm not miserly; in fact, I know only too well I'm a spendthrift. When I hear the cries of the croupiers – 'Trente-et-un, rouge, impair et passe', 'Quatre, noir, pair et manque', it's with a sort of apprehension, a sort of sinking feeling in my heart. How greedily I look at the gaming-table, with its scattered louis d'or, gold friedrichs and thalers, at the streams of gold as they pour from the croupier's hands and pile up into heaps of gold that flash like fire, at the rolls of silver lying around the wheel. Even two rooms away, I can hear the chink of that money, so much so that I almost go into convulsions.

Ah, that evening when I took those seventy gulden to the gaming-table was a memorable one for me. I began by staking ten gulden on passe. I had always had a sort of predilection for passe, but I lost my bet on it. This left me with sixty gulden in silver. After a moment's thought I chose zero, beginning by staking five gulden at a time. Twice I lost, but the third round suddenly brought the coup I longed for. I almost died with joy as I got my hundred and seventy-five gulden. Indeed, I was even more pleased than when I had won the hundred thousand gulden. Wasting no time, I staked another hundred gulden on the red, and won; two hundred on the red, and won; four hundred on the black, and won; eight hundred on manque, and won. Thus, with the addition of the remainder of my original capital, I found myself, within five minutes, in possession of seventeen hundred gulden. Ah, at such moments you forget all your former failures! This I had gained by risking more than my life. I had dared to take the risk, and now, once again, I was in the ranks of men!

I went and took a room, shut myself up in it and sat counting my money until three o'clock in the morning. And when I awoke the next day, I was no longer a servant! I decided to leave at once for Homburg. There I would neither have to serve as a footman nor lie in prison. Half an hour before starting, I went and ventured a couple of stakes, no more than that. The result was that I lost fifteen hundred florins. Nevertheless, I proceeded to Homburg, and have now been here for a month.

Of course, I'm living in a constant state of anxiety now, playing for the smallest of stakes, always on the watch for something to happen, making calculations, standing whole days on end at the gaming-tables just watching the game played – even seeing it in my dreams; but it seems to me that all the while I've grown stiff, as if stuck in mud of some sort. This I conclude from what I experienced in a recent encounter with Mr Astley. I hadn't seen him since we parted at Roulettenburg, and now we had met again quite by accident. I was walking in the public gardens at the time, and thinking about the fact that not only had I still some fifty gulden in my possession, but had also fully paid my hotel bill three days ago. Consequently, I was in a position to try my luck again at roulette, and if I won anything I would be able to continue playing, whereas if I lost what I now had, I would just have to go back to being a footman once again, unless I discovered a Russian family in need of a tutor. Deep in these thoughts, I started on my daily walk through the park and forest towards a neighbouring principality. Sometimes, on such occasions, I spent four hours on the way, and would return to Homburg tired and hungry, but on this particular occasion, I had scarcely left the gardens for the park when I caught sight of Astley sitting on a bench. As soon as he saw me, he called me over and I went and sat down beside him, but as I noticed that he seemed a little stiff in his manner towards me, the feelings of joy which the sight of him had caused were immediately moderated.

'So *you're* here?' he said. 'Well, I had an idea that I would meet you. Don't bother telling me anything, for I know all about it – yes, all about it. In fact, your whole life during the past twenty months is known to me.'

'How closely you watch the activities of your old friends!' I replied. 'That does you immense credit. But wait a moment, you've reminded me of something. Was it you who bailed me out of prison in Roulettenburg when I was in there for a debt of two hundred thalers? *Someone* did.'

'Oh no, it wasn't me! But I did know you were in prison for a debt of two hundred thalers.'

'Perhaps you could tell me who *did* bail me out?'

'No, I'm afraid I couldn't.'

'What an odd thing! I don't know any Russians here, so it can't have been a Russian who befriended me. In Russia we Orthodox folk *do* go bail for one another, but in this case I thought it must have been done by some Englishman or other for some odd reason.'

Mr Astley seemed to be listening to me with some surprise. Evidently he had expected to see me looking more crushed and broken than I was.

'Well,' he said, not very pleasantly, 'I'm nonetheless glad to find that you retain your old independence of spirit, as well as your cheerfulness.'

'Which means that you are annoyed at not having found me more dejected and humiliated than I am?' I replied with a smile.

Astley didn't understand this at first, but presently did so and smiled.

'I like what you say,' he went on. 'In those words I see the clever, triumphant, and, above all, cynical friend of former days. Only Russians have the faculty of combining within themselves so many opposing qualities. Yes, most men love to see their best friend humiliated; generally it is on humiliation that friendship is founded. All thinking people know that ancient truth. Yet, on this present occasion, I assure you, I am sincerely glad to see that you are *not* downcast. Tell me, are you never going to give up gambling?'

'Damn the gambling! Yes, I would certainly give it up, if only—'

'If only you could win back what you've lost? I thought so. You needn't tell me any more. I know how things stand, because what you have just said you said without thinking, and therefore, truthfully. Have you no other employment than gambling?'

'No, none whatsoever.'

Astley started asking me questions. I didn't know anything. It was ages since I had last looked at a paper or turned the pages of a book.

'You're getting rusty,' he said. 'You have not only renounced life, with its interests and social ties, but the duties of a citizen and a man. You have not only given up the friends I know you had, and every aim in life except winning money, but you have also given up your memories. Although I can remember you during the strong, passionate period of your life, I'm persuaded that you have now forgotten all the better feelings you had at that time, and that your present dreams and aspirations do not rise above odd, even, red, black, the twelve middle numbers, and so on.'

'That's enough, Mr Astley!' I exclaimed with some irritation, almost anger. 'Kindly don't bring all that up. I can remember things perfectly well. It's just that I have put them out of my mind for a time. Just until I've got back on my feet. When that time comes, you'll see me rise from the dead.'

'Then you'll be here another ten years,' he replied. 'Should I be alive then, I'll remind you – here, on this very bench – of what I've just said. In fact, I'll make a bet on it.'

'Say no more,' I interrupted impatiently. 'And to show you that I've not wholly forgotten the past, may I ask where Miss Polina is? If it wasn't you who bailed me out of prison, it must have been her. But I've not yet heard a word about her.'

'No, I don't think it was her. At the present moment she's in Switzerland, and you would do me a favour by not asking me questions about her,' Astley said firmly, even angrily.

'Which means that she has dealt you a serious wound too?' I burst out with an involuntary sneer.

'Miss Polina,' he continued, 'is the best of all possible living creatures, but I repeat that I shall thank you to stop questioning me about her. You never really knew her, and her name on your lips is an offence to my moral sensibilities.'

'Indeed? On what subject, then, would I be better to speak to you than on that one? All your memories and mine are linked to it. However, you needn't worry, I have no wish to probe too far into your private and secret affairs. My interest in Miss Polina does not extend beyond her outward circumstances and surroundings. You could tell me about them in a couple of words.'

'Well, on condition that the matter ends there, I'll tell you that Miss Polina was ill for a long time, and still is. My mother and sister looked after her for a while at their home in the north of England. Then Miss Polina's grandmother (you remember the mad old woman?) died, and left her a personal legacy of seven thousand pounds sterling. That was about six months ago, and now Miss Polina is travelling with my sister's family – my sister having since married. Her little brother and sister also benefited in the grandmother's will, and are now being educated in London. As for the General, he died in Paris last month, of a stroke. Mademoiselle Blanche treated him well, but she managed to have all he got from the grandmother transferred to herself. That, I think, is all I have to tell.'

'And how about De Griers? Is *he* travelling in Switzerland too?'

'No, nor do I know where he is. But I warn you once more, you'd better avoid such innuendoes and unworthy suppositions or you'll have me to reckon with.'

'What? In spite of our old friendship?'

'Yes, in spite of our old friendship.'

'Then I beg your pardon a thousand times, Mr Astley. I meant nothing offensive to Miss Polina, for I have nothing to blame her for. Moreover, the question of there being anything between a Frenchman and a Russian lady is not one which you and I need discuss, or even attempt to understand.'

'If,' replied Astley, 'you will refrain from linking these two persons' names, may I ask you to explain what you mean by "a Frenchman", "a Russian lady" and "there being anything between them"? Why are you referring particularly to "a Frenchman" and "a Russian lady"?'

'Ah, so you are interested then, Mr Astley. But it's a long, long story, and calls for a lengthy preface. At the same time, the question is an important one, no matter how ridiculous it may seem at first glance. A Frenchman, Mr Astley, is a fine figure of a man. With this, you, being British, may not agree. As a Russian, I may not agree either, perhaps out of envy. But possibly our good ladies are of another opinion. For instance, you may look on Racine[80] as an artificial, affected, perfumed fellow; you may even find him unreadable; I think the same, and in some respects find him a subject for ridicule. Yet there is a certain charm about him, Mr Astley, and, above all things, he is a great poet, even though you and I might like to deny it. The Frenchman, or as a national representative, the Parisian, was developing into a figure of elegance while we Russians were still no better than bears. The Revolution bequeathed this noble heritage to all Frenchmen, and now every guttersnipe of a Parisian may have manners, modes of expression and thoughts that are above reproach in form, while contributing nothing from his own initiative, intellect or soul – his manners and so on having come to him through inheritance. Under that veneer, the Frenchman is still often an arch-fool and an arch-villain. On the other hand, there is no one in the world more trusting and open than a young Russian lady. A De Griers might so disguise himself and act a part as to easily win her heart, for he has elegance, Mr Astley, and a young lady might easily take that appearance for his real self, for the natural form of his heart and soul, rather than the mere cloak heredity has endowed him with. And even though it may offend you, I feel bound to say that the majority of English people, too, are uncouth and unrefined, whereas we Russian folk can recognise beauty wherever we see it and are always eager to cultivate it. But to distinguish beauty of soul and originality of character needs far more independence and freedom than our women have, especially our younger ladies. At all events, they need more *experience*. For instance, Miss Polina – I beg your pardon, but the name has passed my lips and I cannot take it back – will take a very long time to make up her mind to prefer you to Monsieur de Griers. She may respect you, she may become your friend, she may open her heart to you, but over that heart will be reigning that loathsome villain, that mean and petty usurer, De Griers. This will be due to obstinacy and vanity, to the fact that De Griers once appeared to her in the guise of a marquis, of a disenchanted and ruined liberal who was doing his best to help her family and the frivolous old General; and although these tricks of his have since been exposed, you will find that the exposure has made no impression on her mind. Only give her the De Griers of former days, and she will ask of you no more. The more she may detest the present De Griers, the more will she lament the De Griers of the past, even though the latter only existed in her imagination. You're a sugar refiner, Mr Astley, are you not?'

'Yes, I belong to the well-known firm of Lovell and Co.'

'There you are, then. On the one hand, you're a sugar refiner, while, on the other hand, you're an Apollo Belvedere[81]. But the two characters don't mix with one another. I, for my part, am not even a sugar refiner; I'm a mere gambler at roulette who has also served as a footman. Of this fact Miss Polina is probably well aware, since she appears to have an excellent set of spies at her disposal.'

'You're just saying this because you're feeling bitter,' said Astley coolly. 'There's nothing new in what you're saying.'

'I agree. But the awful thing is that no matter how stale, how hackneyed, how farcical my accusations may be, they are nonetheless *true*. But you and I are getting nowhere.'

'Well, that's because you're just talking nonsense!' exclaimed my companion, his voice now trembling and his eyes flashing. 'You should know,' he continued, 'wretched, unworthy, petty, unfortunate man that you are, that it was at *her* request I came to Homburg, to see you and have a long, serious talk with you and report to her your feelings and thoughts and hopes – yes, and your memories of her, too!'

'Indeed? Is that really so?' I cried, the tears beginning to well from my eyes. (This had never happened to me before.)

'Yes, you unhappy man,' continued Astley. 'She *did* love you, and I can tell you that now because now you are utterly lost. Even if I were also to tell you that she still loves you, you would nonetheless stay where you are. You've ruined yourself beyond redemption. Once upon a time you had a certain amount of talent and a lively personality, and you were quite good-looking too. You might even have been useful to your country, which needs men like you. But you will remain here, and your life is over. I'm not blaming you for this; in my view all Russians are like that, or inclined to be. If it's not roulette, then it's something else. The exceptions are very rare. You aren't the first not to understand what real work is – I'm not talking about your peasants, of course. Roulette is the perfect game for Russians. Up till now, you have honourably preferred to serve as a footman rather than become a thief, but what the future may have in store for you, I tremble to think. Well, goodbye then. You need money, I suppose? Then take these ten louis d'or. I won't give you more than that, because you'll only gamble it away. Take this money, and goodbye. Take it, I say.'

'No, Mr Astley. After all that has been said, I—'

'*Ta – ake* it!' repeated my friend. 'I'm sure you're still a gentleman, and therefore I'm giving you the money as one true friend may always give money to another. If I could be certain that you would leave both Homburg and the gaming-tables, and return to your own country, I would give you a thousand pounds down to start life afresh, but I'm giving you ten louis d'or rather than a thousand pounds because at the present time a thousand pounds and ten louis d'or is all the same to you – you will lose the one amount as easily as you would the other. So take the money, and goodbye.'

'Yes, I *will* take it if at the same time you will embrace me.'

'With pleasure.'

And so we parted, on terms of sincere affection.

But he's wrong. If I was hasty and foolish with regard to Polina and De Griers, *he* was hasty and harsh about Russian people in general. Of myself, I say nothing. But that's all beside the point now. Words are only words. I need to *act*. Above all, I need to think about Switzerland. Tomorrow, tomorrow – Oh, if only I could set off tomorrow, be born again, rise again from the dead! I must show them what I can do. Even if I do no more than prove to Polina that I can still be a man, it would be worth it. It's too late today, but *tomorrow* . . . I have a feeling of expectation, and it can't be wrong. I've got fifteen louis d'or now, though I only began with fifteen gulden. If I play carefully to start with . . . But no! Surely I'm not such a fool as that. I'm a lost soul. But why should I *not* rise from the dead? All I need to do is play cautiously and patiently at first and the rest will follow. All I need to do is keep control of myself for one hour, and my destiny will be changed forever. The key thing is character. I only have to remember what happened to me some months ago at Roulettenburg, before I was finally ruined. What a notable instance that was of how determined I can be! On that occasion I had lost everything – everything; but, just as I was leaving the casino, I heard one single gulden rattling in my pocket. 'Well, at least I can get something to eat,' I thought to myself; but a hundred paces further on, I changed my mind and went back in. I staked that gulden on manque – and there is definitely something strange, when you're alone, in a foreign land and far from your home and friends, with no idea where your next meal is coming from, to be nevertheless staking your very last coin! Well, I won, and twenty minutes later left the casino with a hundred and seventy gulden in my pocket! That's a fact, and it shows what one last remaining gulden can do . . . But what if my courage had failed me? What if I hadn't dared to make that decision? . . .

Tomorrow. Tomorrow it will all be over!

NOTES

1   *Uchitel* is Russian for 'teacher' or 'tutor'. In the Russian text, the word is written with a French spelling, *outchitel.*

2   A *table d'hôte* is a table in a hotel or restaurant where the guests are seated together for the meal provided, as opposed to a table for a private party.

3   'That wasn't so foolish.'

4   General Perovsky described in his *Memoirs* French soldiers in 1812 shooting the ill and exhausted in a column of Russian prisoners of war.

5   Dostoyevsky refers to the money as both 'gulden' and 'florins'. The coins are Dutch guilders, which were often called florins.

6   'Of a disreputable kind'.

7   A louis d'or is a coin worth 20 francs.

8   German for 'father'.

9   The Rothschild and Hoppe families were bankers.

10 In Imperial Russia, a knout was a whip used to administer punishments.

11 'Baroness, I have the honour to be your slave.'

12 'Yes indeed!'

13 'Are you mad?'

14 'But the Baron is so irascible, a Prussian type, he'll start a quarrel just for the sake of it.' There is a play on words in the French that is not conveyed by the English translation: 'querelle d'Allemand' is literally 'quarrel of a German'; so we have a 'Prussian type' starting a 'German quarrel'.

15 'Good grief!'

16 A 'jumped-up nobody'.

17 A family of Italian nobility.

18 The basilisk is a mythical creature whose look could kill.

19 'Yes, Madame. And, believe me, I'm so delighted. Your health . . . it's a miracle . . . seeing you here. A charming surprise.'

20 'The old lady is in her second childhood.'

21 'Why, madame, that will be a pleasure.'

22 'But she's in her second childhood. Left on her own, she'll do something stupid.'

23 'Leave, leave!'

24 A friedrich d'or or gold friedrich was a Prussian coin, worth ten gulden or florins.

25 'Place your bets, gentlemen! Place your bets, gentlemen! No more bets?'

26 'How much zero? Twelve? Twelve?'

27 'No more bets!'

28 'What a victory!'

29 'But, Madame, that was brilliant!'

30 'Princess . . . a poor emigrant . . . constant misfortune . . . Russian princes are so generous.'

31 'Hell! She's a dreadful old woman.'

32 'What the Devil is that?'

33 'But, madame, luck can change, one bit of bad luck and you will lose everything . . . especially with the way you bet . . . it was awful!'

34 'You're bound to lose.'

35 'Oh, that's not the point. My dear sir, the general is wrong.'

36 'To this poor, awful old woman'.

37 'Hell, that's not the way, that's not the way.'

38 'Oh my dear Mr Alexei, be so kind.'

39 'What a shrew!'

40 'We will drink milk, on the fresh grass.'

41 'Nature and truth'; a quotation from Rousseau.

42 'Oh, hell.'

43 'She'll live to be a hundred!'

44 Paul de Kock (1793–1871) was a French novelist.

45 'The old Russian countess, who was in her second childhood.'

46 Like French, Russian has two words for 'you' when addressing one person, one of which is more formal and the other used more

with family and friends. Up till this point, Polina has used the more formal pronoun вы (comparable to French 'vous') when talking to Alexei, but now she is using the more intimate ты (comparable to French 'tu').

47 'The last three goes, gentlemen.'

48 The first professional female balloonist, Sophie Blanchard died in 1819 when her balloon caught fire and she fell to the ground.

49 'The gentleman has already won a hundred thousand florins.'

50 'Oh, it's him!! Come in, then, you silly thing! Is it true that you've won a mountain of gold and silver? I'd prefer the gold.'

51 My pet, how silly you are! . . . We'll have a party, won't we?'

52 'My son, have you got courage?'

53 'Anyone else . . .' Pierre Corneille was a 17th-century French dramatist.

54 ' . . . if you're not too silly, I'll take you to Paris.'

55 'Well, if you like, you shall see Paris. Anyway, what's a "tutor"? You were really stupid when you were a "tutor".'

56 'Well, what'll you do if I take you with me? . . . And I'll make you see stars in broad daylight.'

57 ' . . . I'm a good-natured girl . . . but you'll see stars.'

58 'Abject slave!'

59 'And after that, the flood.' This is a rewording of *Après nous, le déluge* (After us, the flood') attributed to Madame de Pompadour, the mistress of Louis XV of France, but also attributed to Louis himself in the form *Après moi, le déluge*. In other words, 'after us/me, it doesn't matter what happens'.

60 'But you can't understand that! . . . Hey, what are you doing?'

61 'Very well, my "tutor". I'll be waiting for you, if you want.'

62 ' . . . and you'll be as happy as a little king.'

63 'As for me, I want an allowance of fifty thousand francs, and then—'

64 'And as for the hundred thousand francs we have left, you'll squander them with me, my uchitel.'

65 'He's an uchitel who's won two hundred thousand francs . . .'

66 'You've got the spirit to understand. You know, my lad, . . .'
67 'But – you know – but, tell me . . .? But you know . . . What will
    you do after this, then?'
68 'Yes, yes, that's it, that's wonderful . . . You know . . . because I
    thought you were nothing but an "uchitel" (that's something like
    a servant, isn't it?) . . . because I'm a kind-hearted girl.'
69 'We've all got to get through being young.'
70 'You're a real philosopher, do you know that? Yes, a real philoso-
    pher. Well, I'll love you, then, I'll love you. You'll see, you'll be
    happy.'
71 'A real Russian, a Kalmyk.'
72 The Bal Mabille was a fashionable dancing establishment
    constructed like gardens and sumptuously decorated.
73 A former royal palace and gardens in Paris.
74 Incoherently
75 'He's in luck.'
76 'Very proper.'
77 'He does really look very proper.'
78 'You were an easy-going fellow . . . I thought you were stupid,
    and you seemed to be . . .'
79 'We will always be good friends . . . and you will be happy.'
80 Jean Racine, 17th-century French dramatic poet.
81 A famous marble statue of the Greek and Roman god Apollo, long
    considered an example of aesthetic perfection.